VOICES OF THE SOUTH

THE INKLING

THE INKLING

FRED CHAPPELL

LOUISIANA STATE UNIVERSITY PRESS   *Baton Rouge*

07 06 05 04 03 02 01 00 99 98   5 4 3 2 1

Library of Congress Cataloging-in-Publication Data
Chappell, Fred, 1936–
    The inkling / Fred Chappell.
    p.   cm. — (Voices of the South)
    ISBN 0-8071-2317-X (alk. paper)
    1. Boys—North Carolina—Psychology—Fiction.   2. Family—North
Carolina—Fiction.   I. Title.   II. Series.
PS3553.H298I18   1998
813'.54—dc21   98-24403
                                                                          CIP

DEDICATED TO *the Jim Applewhites*
AND TO *the Robert Watsons*
AND TO THE MEMORY OF *Herman Ziegner*

Monstru horrendu, informe, ingens,
cui lumen ademptum

THE INKLING

ONE

A YOUNG MAN, sixteen years old, was sitting hunkered on his heels in a stretch of tall yellow sagegrass.
His hair was yellow like the sagegrass and the slight
down sprinkled on his jaws and down his neck was yellow. And his tan windbreaker had faded from foul
weather until it too was almost the color of sagegrass, just
slightly darker. The wind moved in the sage and worried
it over, and the young man did not move except now
and then to tip back his head when he drank from the
dark bottle. The liquor was yellow and flamed in his
throat. The fellow was hunkered in the field, fiercely
self-willed; he was like a belligerent voice.

The sun was high and hot, the color of the sagegrass, but the breeze had a cold edge on it. It was early October. The maple leaves were ruby-colored, the beech trees jerked in the wind like giant candle flames, yellow and transitory. In the clear sharp air the mountains seemed to have drifted forward, nearer now without the summer haze. The mountains were spattered with red, yellow, and blue over green. The premonitory wind had polished the sky clear as a lens.

He was drunk. In the yellowed windbreaker his chest swam in sweat and the hair on the back of his neck was damp. In his steel-rimmed spectacles (the lenses of which did not magnify), the reflected sagegrass moved restlessly and in the corner of each glass square the sun was a tiny yellow dot, the size of the pupils of his eyes. His mind was filled with yellow light and with his own presence. So weightily he existed in the field that he might have created it. When he tipped his head back the muscles in his neck distended to the size of fingers. He drank again; again.

Across a trickling ditch about thirty yards before him there was no sagegrass, but a cool smooth lawn in the deep shadow of an oak tree, A swing made of an old automobile tire went back and forth, and the female child swinging uttered mindless whoops. Her pink dress was no longer stiff with starch and it fluttered in the wind. Her legs were skinny and dirty. She swung wildly, shrieking, and already there was much in her voice that was unchildlike.

Near the swing stood the child's brother, a year younger than she, six years old. He too was blond, his hair brighter than the sagegrass, almost silvery. His movements were slow and deliberate as he tossed a base-

4

ball gently into the air and lashed at it with a dull-colored bat. When he knocked it some yards away he walked to pick it up; he went slowly and then carried it back to his position under the tree to hit it again.

At last he fouled the ball behind him. It went spinning, arcing up over the ditch and over a pond of the shadowy sagegrass. It fell and rolled forward a few feet and came to rest a yard or so before the yellow-haired fellow. He stared at it. It lay solid and self-contained, disputing his supremacy of existence in the field. He stared at it malevolently.

The boy watched the ball, and when it fell the young man could see from where he sat hunkered that the boy uttered a huge sigh. His thin shoulders rose; fell. With much difficulty he stopped the swing and helped his sister squeeze through the tire. Grasping her hand he led her to the gurgling ditch and they went down. In a moment they bobbed up again like swimmers and came forward. The girl was whimpering and the boy was reassuring her and he told her quietly to hush, keeping his voice low and steady as if he was calming a skittish mare. Still leading her, the boy began making wide steady arcs, watching his feet closely. The yellow-haired fellow watched the ball lying stubborn before him, stiffly resisting being found. He held the bottle in his left hand and did not drink; his right hand was red, wound about with a blood-soaked crude bandage. He did not move as they came closer, and it was clear that they were going to find the ball at last, although they had not yet seen him.

He stood, rising quickly from his hunkered position, as quickly as a knife blade flicked open. He towered over them, looking yellow and wild. He bent and scooped up the ball and held it aloft, and it was almost hidden in his

5

white hand. He had shifted the liquor bottle to his wounded right hand. They retreated a few steps, the boy dragging the girl back, getting her behind himself. They both were white and so fearful they might have trembled out of existence like match flames.

"Hanh, you goddam kids!" he cried. He shook the ball in his hand. "What if you was to die? What if you was to die one day?" he cried.

The boy looked so fierce from fear that he looked like a trapped fox. He snatched a glance behind him into the cool smooth lawn; no one was there.

"One day; what if you was to die one day?" he cried. "Hanh! Hanh!" He threw the ball away into the air. It landed in the lawn, rolling forward fast to bounce against the oak tree. "Hanh! Hanh!" The yellow-haired man was laughing and shouting. *Hanh!* He strode toward them, whipping through the sagegrass, and went past them. He shifted the bottle back into his unwounded left hand. He had to clamber on his hands and knees up the bank to the roadbed because he was afraid of dropping the bottle. As soon as he had begun to walk he felt cooler.

The boy held tightly to his sister's arms above her elbows. She was trying to strike him, to scratch him, and she was gulping air in great murderous sobs. He kept trying to soothe her, to lead her back into the green lawn.

Then a year later almost the same thing happened. The mother and the uncle had gone off to town on some necessary errand. It was later in the season, November or December, and a silent disquieting snow lay everywhere. The smooth lawn was smoother still and it looked like a huge linen tablecloth. A smear of snow was on the bottom rim of the tire swing like a smudge of beard on a round face. They were playing in the living room around the chocolate-colored oil heater which boomed like an uncertain drum when the boy spanked it with an open hand. His sister's eyes were always on him, fearfully trusting. Now she was taller and stronger than he. They were playing together with unaccustomed noise so that at the beginning they did not hear the terrifying voice.

She heard it first. "Jan, Ja-an," she said.

He gazed at her, baffled, silent.

"It's *them*," she said. "I can hear them talking."

"No," he said. "It's not them. You can't hear them."

But then in a moment it really was as if it were the dead people talking. The low terrifying note, wordlessly questioning, sounded in the room, thrilling through the very walls of the house.

"Yes it is," she breathed. She began to cry silently, tears welling and remaining bright in her eyes.

The low cold note sounded twice again.

"No," he whispered, "it's not the dead ones talking." He tore himself from a momentary trance and ran to the door and slammed it open. White coldness flooded his whole body instantly and he shuddered. *Croo, croo.* From the bare oak tree, on a branch above the still O of the swing, the little gray owl looked at him with mean yellow eyes. "It's an owl," he said.

She was behind him in the doorway. The tears were streaking down her feverish cheeks. "Who is it, Jan? What are they saying?"

Croo, crrrooo.

"It's just a squinch owl. He can't hurt you."

The owl blinked as suddenly as a man would snap his fingers. It cocked its head to one side and Timmie thought that it was trying to get a better look at her. "I

7

see it," she said. "Won't it go away? Make it go away, Jan."

"Shoo!" he cried, waggling his thin arms up and down. *Croo.*

He ran out into the yard and scooped up snow and packed it, slapping it tight with both hands. The first snowball he threw went far away, not even touching the tree; the second ball splashed on the black tree trunk, making a shape like he and Timmie made when they squeezed a drop of ink in a creased paper. Looking slow, the little owl toppled forward, the long wings outspread. It came swooping low toward him over the smooth snow.

"Jan, watch out! Jan, don't let it get you!" She ran shrieking into the house, through the dark living room.

He ducked, crossing his thin forearms over his head and the back of his neck. The owl passed far overhead, wheeling up suddenly at the corner of the roof, and then beating its wings stoutly as it flew away through the gelid air. He watched it until it was a mere dot and lost among the spiny branches of the woods toward the east. He went into the house and closed the door, leaning the back of his head against it for a moment while his chest palpitated with jagged breathing. Through two closed doors he could hear a dim moaning. At the door to the hall he paused; the moaning had grown louder, and he was scared he might frighten her to death. "It's me," he said loudly. "It's Jan, Timmie; it's me." He went in and found her in their own small bedroom, lying on the floor behind the bed on the other side of the room. She was clutching a giant stuffed giraffe to her. She pressed the dumb head to her belly and had thrown her skinny legs over the soiled neck of the toy. The whole top of her dress front was wet from her crying.

8

"Hush, Timmie," he said. "Don't keep on crying and crying."

She would not stop; she couldn't stop until much later, when the mother and the uncle returned.

TWO

"Hush, just hush," said Uncle Hake. "I don't want to hear any more about it."

Jan scooted over the worn wool rug; he had designed something important to build with the Tinkertoys.

Uncle Hake had once told the mother: "I ain't no daddy, I ain't no family man. You better stick to your guns and find some guy that will take care of you, some guy that wants a ready-made family." He rattled the newspaper with a great deal of useless verve. Uncle Hake smoked terrible cheap cigars. Uncle Hake was glum, uninterested, rather stupid. Hard to imagine how he and the mother were of the same family.

He was short, slightly slouched always, his shoulders rounded, his hair gone now; large-jointed all over: he was a funny-looking knobby little man. His nose too was rounded like a ball of dough, and beneath it he wore a dark little bristly mustache. He would sit in the flowery easy chair near the oil heater and rattle the newspaper and if Jan or Timmie came near enough he would very quickly take off his slipper—it was his one deft move— and slap the children across the arms or legs or chest. Every evening and all day Saturday and Sunday he would make quick nervous trips to the bathroom, and each time he returned his breath smelled ever more sweetly and fiery. Once or twice a week the mother forgot and asked him to carry out the garbage; and then he would scrooch his eyebrows down until his whole face was a squeezed lump like an angry fist and he would say, "Why don't you get these damn trifling kids learned to do a little something?" And he would hunt through the house, his greasy bedroom slipper in his hand, until he found them. Swat, swat. "You kids better learn to do a little something to earn your keep around here."

He labored at the crossword puzzles in the newspaper, mumbling and chewing at the frayed corners of the mustache.

Summer mornings he would sit out in the cool smooth lawn in the crooked rocking chair, rocking away. He was barefoot and wore old greasy gray trousers and a yellowed undershirt with thin straps that kept slipping off his round shoulders. Then he was drunk plainly enough; on hot summer nights he couldn't sleep and all night he bumbled about in his dingy little room, mumbling and drinking and gnawing at the bristly corners of the mustache. Wouldn't he at last eat it all away? If he could be

11

zipped open down the front, it was certain there would be a great ball of hair in his stomach, as in a cow's.

Everyone got along with Uncle Hake without respecting or loving him. This was because for everyone he knew he existed only as a sort of chip in a tooth which the tongue is always unconsciously seeking: embarrassingly familiar, faintly annoying, but always reassuring. As long as Uncle Hake was around you knew the universe was still identical with the one you had always known: it had not suddenly been cleansed overnight.

Timmie treated Uncle Hake with a half-fearful reverence, the way she treated all inanimate objects. Jan, who spent all his time training his will, found it easiest to ignore his uncle, not wasting his energy on what was after all an unusable lump. Anyway, what if Uncle Hake had no real will to exercise against?

He had a number of cronies who were all as lugubriously out of kilter as he. They were either short and pudgy and greasy or long and scrawny and sallow, and they had names like Pete or Johnny or Jake. They didn't come to the house very often, but Jan learned to despise the sight and smell of them; Timmie of course ran quickly away to hide, peering out unexpectedly. They wore red or bright blue neckties, these old men, and the knot was never correct but hard and tight, and their breaths reeked with alcohol like painted sores. Uncle Hake sometimes played poker with them, going stubbornly off Friday evenings as the mother watched tightmouthed, and returning in the deepest hours of the morning. He was extraordinarily unlucky, but now and again he won, and then the two children would find him strutting about the lawn in the morning, without a shirt and barefoot in the iron-colored dew, the ash of his fumy cigar growing always longer and droopier.

On the wall in his dingy room was a picture of a big blond lady in one of the new very small bathing suits. The photograph Jan peeked at fearfully at first, and then later on, belligerently. There were on his dresser three greasy combs and a box of the rank cigars. On a small table by the door were a fountain pen and a pencil stub and a stack of bills, of which Uncle Hake paid a single one every day until the stack was gone. Then the new bills came in. It was merely that he somehow felt that in writing only one check each day he was spending less money than if he paid all the bills at once. He kept all receipts, binding them in thick packets with rubber bands. Trying as hard as she could, the mother could do nothing toward making the room cheery. And Uncle Hake would have possessed a Spartan existence except that he lived in the languorous luxury of blind ignorance, irritatedly unknowing. He did not even really keep up with the war news. In this dim room the lady in the bikini began by being explosively present, but with the months her picture got darker and darker; she too was being ignominiously stained by Uncle Hake, like one of his undershirts.

And he would lounge about for weeks—or months or years if it had been possible—in the same greasy yellowish clothes without changing. The mother would say, "Hake, let me have those clothes and I'll put them in the wash I've got to do today." Uncle Hake would say, "Aw, leave me alone and quit pestering me. I guess I can change my own clothes. You're always pestering me about something, you won't never give me any peace." It turned out finally that she always had to wake up early and sneak into his room and steal his clothes off the bedpost to get them washed. He complained about that too—he was continually complaining about everything, of course, but no one paid him any mind. It was like the noise of traffic at night when you were trying to sleep: you finally got so accustomed to it you didn't hear it any more.

And it was a silly accident that kept him out of the war: when he was seventeen years old he had dropped a sledge hammer on his left foot. (He had never again picked one up.)

And he worked in a laboratory in the paper mill, testing for the chemical qualities of paper, and he hated the job with a dull and constant hate.

THREE

Jan had begun when he was very young—perhaps when he was five years old—to test his will, to flex it. He had begun merely by trying to outstare Buddha, the gray-and-black-striped mongrel cat. Everyday he spent long hours looking into those feline sardonic slitted eyes, and his will grew equally in heat as it grew in strength and intensity until finally he acquired a hateful contempt for this particular object. The cat was bored in the beginning but gradually became afraid, and then one day after some weeks of this staring it looked away. Jan was maliciously joyful. He rose from his squat and reached and gathered the cat into his arms. Across the trickling ditch he took it, into the sagegrass which swirled about his waist, pecking at his warmly laden wrists. By a largish rock he set the cat on the ground and placed his foot lightly upon it, and he raised the stone and flung it down upon the cat's head. Buddha screeched, a horrid loud baby-like shrieking, but there was no one in the house except Timmie, who was asleep. No one stopped Jan or called to him. Again; again; again, he flung the stone down and the cat fought desperately beneath his foot, taking a long time to die. But at last he had killed it and he grasped the dead Buddha by the tail and swung it away into a squirmy bank of honeysuckle. The stone he took up and carried back from the field to the house and put down near the back door. It was smeared on one awkward side with blood and there were other, whitish, stains here and there upon it. It was to be a new obstacle for him to vanquish; and in time he came to know every mark, the contour of every stain, each minuscule protuberance, the vague course of every vein, every tiny pit in the texture of the surface. He squatted before it, gazing hotly, and it looked as if he might be worshiping a god in the stone. This time he managed the exercise without gathering rancor and he and the stone in the end became brothers, and Jan was satisfied that he had overcome the will of the stone without having to displace it. Yet despite this truce Jan was a fiery wild being. Under the very blond hair which fell over his forehead his eyes were always scarily direct, as blunt as two fingers. It seemed that all that willed puissance had lodged in the eyes.

Thus, even at a young age, he had made a great part of the world he knew embarrassedly aware of him—and more. With those eyes he could catch things in the off-balance moment, or force things off balance himself. Over and over Uncle Hake said to him, "Stop cuttin' them old eyes at me, boy." Swat, with the slipper. Jan shrugged him off as if he were a horsefly. But the uncle's discomfiture about the boy was inescapable, and he found himself avoiding Jan as much as possible; but Uncle Hake avoided everyone, such a dim dingy life he led anyway. The mother watched Jan going bored and purposeful through the house and she kept wondering, wondering.

He kept long hours to himself in the dusty garret or in the disused barn. He sat thinking, watching cool yellow slats of light creep slowly off the floor and higher across the walls. He watched insects crawl along in the dust, and mice would play over his feet sometimes, so long he sat still. From three or four window screens and odd pieces of wood he built a cage—he was seven or eight years old then—and caught the mice, desperate and feverish, in his hands and dropped them in. He fed them on what he could steal from the pantry or the garbage can, and one day he brought Timmie out to the barn to have a look. There were a dozen or so of the gray mice, roiling together in the little rusty cage. In the slant yellow light their eyes were iridescent little red circles.

Timmie advanced; scuttled back. She clutched his arm.

"I'm going to keep on saving them up," he told her seriously, "and one night after they're good and hungry I'm going to take them into Uncle Hake's room and turn them loose on him. When we wake up that morning there won't be nothing left of Uncle Hake but a big pile of old bones." From his pocket he produced half a soda cracker and held it dramatically between thumb and forefinger. Quickly he opened the top of the cage and dropped the cracker crumb among them. They rushed to it instantly. *Keerk, keerk, keek, keek.*

She watched with great round eyes and dug her fingers into his arm. "Don't do it, Jan," she said. "That's bad. Don't do that."

"Nothin' but just a pile of old bones," he said.

"Don't do it, Jan. Please." Now she didn't cry, but she watched wide-eyed until the cracker disappeared.

And then that night she had a nightmare and she was racked with shuddery convulsive vomiting. She shrieked again and again as the mother bent over her, holding her wet forehead gently and patting her hands. "There there," she said, "there now, there there. It's all right, baby; it's all right, honey." She cleaned the girl's neck and pajama blouse with different washcloths. Jan thought that she would crazily let it out about his mice, but all the mother could get from her was something about "a long bony man."

"It was a big long bones," said Timmie, choking. Her face was white as salt.

"A man?" asked the mother.

"Yes," cried Timmie. "A big long bones man."

"A long bony man," the mother said. She sighed. "There now, honey, it's all right. You're going to be all right."

Jan moved his legs luxuriously under the sheet. It was so late and dark outside that the overhead light in the room seemed brighter than he'd ever seen it. The big stuffed giraffe had tumbled off her bed, foully spattered.

After a long while the mother was satisfied and went away, enjoining them to keep quiet and go to sleep. She clicked out the light, leaving them darkling in the separate beds.

Jan waited until he heard her enter her own room down the hall. "Timmie?" he asked.

At first she wouldn't answer.

"Timmie," he said, "don't be afraid about it. I was just teasing you. I was just kidding."

"Are you going to put them on him?" Her voice was throaty, rich with dread.

"No, I'm not going to. I was just fooling."

"I'm glad then," she said simply. "Because it would be bad."

"Yes." He realized at that moment that he would have to look out for Timmie, to take care of her. Though she was larger and taller than he, and a year older, he was much stronger in a way that seemed to be important. It was strange to think about in the dark late night with her beside him still lying awake, afraid. In the window eight or nine pale stars glittered relentlessly.

Next day he hid the mice in a different corner in the barn, covering the cage over with some old straw and some rotten burlap, so that Timmie wouldn't run across it accidentally. Later on he would go about the house collecting sharp pointed instruments, pencils, paring knives, and he would throw them away. He would break the points off scissors that were left lying about. He never wondered why the mother or the uncle—well, Uncle Hake; what could be expected?—showed so little wisdom about Timmie. He saw that even the mother was blind on one whole side, gentle and knowing as she was.

He shrugged. His bony shoulders rose; fell. He stood at the window, gazing out into the yard. In the big oak tree an oriole's nest, pear-shaped, bobbed free in the breeze. In an orange ray of light that got through the branches a gang of midges danced brightly, golden atoms. Something twinkled on the lawn, and when he looked closer he saw that it was a snake. "It's a big chunkhead," he said solemnly. He went to check on Timmie. She was in their bedroom, trying to stuff the soiled giraffe into a dresser drawer. Then he went out to look. Sure enough, it was a big copperhead, which drew back into a taut trembling S when it felt him coming. He looked about for something to kill it with, but then thought of Uncle Hake. On a deliberated impulse he decided to tell the uncle about the snake.

He went straight in. Uncle Hake was lying on the bed in his dim room, wearing dark greasy trousers and a yellowed undershirt. "Damn it, boy," he said, "ain't you learned no better than to bust in without knocking? If it was mine to do, I'd whack some goddam sense in your head."

"There's a big snake out in the yard."

"A big snake, huh?" His eyes were dull and his breath was hot with liquor. "What kind?"

"It's a big chunkhead," Jan said.

"Chunkhead, huh? Has it got a spot like a penny on the back of the head?"

"Yes."

"I guess it's a chunkhead then." He raised himself painfully to a sitting position. "You go out and keep it there," he said. "I'll be there in a minute." With his bare soiled feet he felt about on the floor for his shoes. "Don't let it get away."

"All right."

Surprisingly, the snake had not got much farther. Jan stood about five feet away and stamped hard on the ground. The snake hissed, flexed into a coil. He looked at it uncaring: it was merely a big snake.

Uncle Hake came around the corner of the house. He

slouched along, one thin strap of the undershirt flopping on his arm as he walked. In his right hand, held loosely at his shambling thigh, he carried a big nickel-plated revolver. Jan's attention fastened significantly on the pistol. It was something he hadn't known about, hadn't actually expected. He determined on the spot to make a close examination of Uncle Hake's room as soon as possible. The uncle raised the pistol and aimed it shakily at the dully glowing head of the snake. He missed with the first shot, spraying the ground to the left of the snake up into a little jet. The snake hissed again and spread out of the coil like oil oozing over a hard surface, and then drew back again into the tense quivering S. Uncle Hake fired again; he shot away the copper-colored head. Then he breathed unevenly and lowered the gun and dropped the cylinder open and shook the bullets into his left hand. The bullets he put into his left pocket, stuffing the gun into the other. "Get rid of that goddam thing, boy," he told Jan.

"All right." Unconsciously Jan kept looking at the lumpy bulge of the uncle's trousers pocket.

"And stop cuttin' them old eyes around at me, damn you."

"All right."

Uncle Hake turned his back on Jan and walked away, trying to square back his round shoulders, pulling up the slipped strap of the undershirt with a greasy thumb.

Jan picked up the crazy wriggling headless snake and took it over to the ditch, dropped it into the little oily stream that trickled at the bottom. The body thrashed wildly in the water, turning up the sickening white underbelly again and again. The brackish water began to tinge pink. . . . And he had found out about the gun. He had also discovered that Uncle Hake had been scared of the snake and—maybe—of the gun too. He mulled the thought, scratching his armpit. Yes, it was true: the uncle was frightened of his own pistol.

Two days later he found the opportunity and he searched the room, going through all the drawers and the closet and even looking under the bed. He found the pistol right enough and only one other thing he hadn't counted on, a fairly large tan-colored book of photographs of men and women doing silly things among each other, all of them hairy and huge between the legs. The book smelled musky and queer. It took him a good while to figure out how to get the cylinder of the gun open, but finally he managed, and shook three bullets from the chambers onto the bedspread. He examined them closely, looking at them over and over. They were heavier than he had thought, and this was a distinct disadvantage. He shrugged; it was just something he would have to chance. Taking fine care he replaced everything. He surveyed the room. Had he obliterated his tracks? He was satisfied. He had left no trace.

And then it took about three weeks to whittle out the phony bullets properly. He carved them from hard splintery locust wood, kneading them in a bag of fine sand to make them smooth. The blunt noses of them he colored with pencil lead. He colored with white crayon the jackets; they didn't shine as they ought, but this was another chance he had counted on taking. The brass-colored caps in the butts of the jackets were fashioned of clay mixed with a drop of red fingernail polish. He hefted the finished fakes; they were crude. They would have to do. He shrugged. The first chance he got he made the substitution, poking the wooden bullets into the same chambers he had taken the real ones from. Wrapping the actual bullets in a scrap of brown paper, he hid them behind a loose board in a stall in the abandoned barn. He strode from the barn into the cold sunlight, grinning. Now Uncle Hake didn't have to be scared of his pistol any more.

FOUR

TIMMIE KNEW, but darkly and thinly, that she had come through all right, that the long time of helplessly placing her trust entirely in Jan had been rewarded. Though it required only a part of his attention, he had begun to protect her. With him it was always better; she managed partly to forget how the things kept trying to get at her. Only her brother and Jannie, the huge stuffed giraffe, were reliable. The mother was a good cool comfort, with her smooth white face and her full eyes, but there wasn't enough of her. When she was present it was as if she had been lowered through the roof and soon would be jerked up again; she kept seeming to descend

24

to aid and too soon rising away. But Jan stayed close. When the gray little wad of a bird stopped on the fence and glared at her with the bad glassy eye that would sometimes go white and blind for an instant, Jan kept it from darting on her and boring into her chest with its beak. He kept the blue mountains with the legs as big as houses from crushing her. Even when he was not immediately with her, it was all right in the house and, especially, in their bedroom, because he would be with her soon. Then he would go off again, looking around him. He was always looking at things. When the two loud booms had happened out in the lawn, he had come into the bedroom in a few minutes. He had raised her from the floor behind her bed and cooed to her, always stroking the long brown hair the mother had made pretty for her. "There there, there there," he said.

The mother kept looking at Jan; her big brown eyes were steady on Jan, and she turned her head toward him when he went walking straight and firm through the house, his hands in his pockets, always glancing everywhere about himself. Jan and the mother were tied somehow, by being together or apart. It was hard to think about. Timmie watched the mother watching Jan, who went on autonomously, like a car that would not hurt her. It was his way. The bright light in her bedroom and the white curtains with the red and yellow spots were tied too, together or apart. It was hard to think about. For sureness she hugged Jannie to her, thrusting his mottled neck tightly between her legs.

Jan called Jannie Ralph Giraffe, always smiling; he didn't know she had already named the animal Jannie.

Swat, swat: she heard it from the living room. Jan had passed near Uncle Hake's chair, but he hadn't paused because of the slaps and she heard his steady tread as he came on through and down the hall. Quickly she went to the wall. She placed her heels against the base of the wall and kept her back and her head hard against it and waited. Jan opened the door and looked and when he saw her standing that way he came on in. "Hey there, Timmie," he said.

She giggled. It was nice the way he always talked to her: softly, with his coolly warm voice.

"How you doing there, Timmie?"

Totally delighted, she skipped away from the wall and threw herself gently on her bed. She peeked smiling around the veil of her long hair, which had fallen over her face. Then she was intent and serious. "Is Uncle Hake bad, Jan?" she asked.

Jan was serious too. "No, he's not bad. He's just joking."

"Is he joking to hit you like that? Is he bad?"

"No," he declared, "he's just kidding us. He don't mean anything." Ten thousand times now he must have told her this.

She was mollified. She turned on her back in the bed and leaned down and got the big stuffed giraffe. She held it in the air above her, singing, "Now, now, there-now, there-now." She sang in a clear moony voice.

He saw that she was happy and, satisfied, he wandered off again.

She sang to Jannie a long while; then, nestling the toy against her, she fell into a sunny doze. Her sleep was muzzy with great piles of white clouds suffused brightly with the big mirror-colored sun. Bright pinkish threads were alive in the clouds and drifted and crept about, working steadily to the music of a clear treble wordless song. This was her own voice made huge. The clouds bulged inward, burning with a bright blue, and the scalloped edges began to lap forward, gradually turning dark. And now all the clouds had turned dark, deeply black, and now a big wind had sprung up, and the clouds were blown away, dispersing quickly in misty rags, revealing the blank uncolored sky behind. In the sky a great naked pair of feet floated, incandescent and bright as the amorphous clouds had been. Timmie's dream eyes stared at the feet for a very long while. Finally on the white center of each foot there bloomed a small rose, red as fire.

She opened her eyes slowly, coming awake. Her nose was white with beadlets of sweat; she had been sleeping directly in the sunlight which poured through the open windows. Now a breeze had entered, raising as gently as wings the curtains with the red and yellow spots. Not all of the dream was so happy; there had been bad places that she didn't wish to think of. With vigorous circular motions she rubbed the moisture off her face and then rubbed her hands on her pretty white dress, leaving slight gray smears at her hips. She rose and walked a bit stiffly—her soft rectangular body oscillated from side to side—to the door and peered out. Uncle Hake had left the flowered easy chair by the oil heater; she knew he was lounging in his room. She went quietly into the living room and looked out the window. No one was in the yard, no one in the heavy smothering shade of the tree. But there was Jan, coming out of the barn, grinning. She smiled to see his grin, for he never smiled that she knew about except when he was purposefully in her presence. Now he emerged grinning from the black maw of the barn.

The cool yellow sunlight was beginning to straggle off behind the dark mountain now; the light was a bright yellow, the color of Jan's hair. She felt that he didn't know it yet, but his hair was no longer so very white, sugar-colored. It was a brilliant stark yellow, sheeny as silk.

He was coming to the house. She turned from the window regretfully. Unknowingly she now was seeking fear, a slight fear. Unthinkingly she wanted more and more of the comfort that was in Jan, more of his sureness. Behind her she heard the familiar clatter in the kitchen and she hurried back toward their bedroom; all the bustle that was necessary in the preparation of the evening meal bothered her.

Yet she had felt what she had felt, and that night there was another, different crisis with her. She tried to feign the horripilative awakening this time. After having lain in the other twin bed for what seemed many hours (but it was not really late; the mother was still awake and stirring), she rose on her elbows shrieking, forcing out dry coughs. The mother came, and, *snick*, turned on the bright bedroom light. Timmie looked at Jan, who had turned to her, half rising himself, groggy but with his face filled with staring concern. When she saw his worried expression Timmie couldn't help her glad smile. But when she smiled Jan's eyes changed and his face went stiff and alert.

"There now, honey, what's wrong now?" the mother asked.

"I had a bad dream," said Timmie.

"Are you all right, baby?"

"It was a long bony man," Timmie said. She was still smiling, her voice was happy.

"Now now, it's all right. You're all right, sweetheart. You go to sleep now. You can go to sleep all right, can't you?"

"Well," said Timmie. She lay down and pulled the sheet up under her chin. She was helplessly grinning, stealing quick glances at Jan.

"You go on to sleep now, baby," the mother said. She snapped off the light and closed the door and they heard her sharp footsteps going away down the hall.

It was a long time before he spoke. "Timmie."

She heard the bad overtone of his voice and she wouldn't answer.

"Timmie."

She sighed silently, but she had to move a bit in the bed, and he heard the creak of the springs.

"Timmie, I don't want you to do that again, all right? If you do like that, I won't know when it's true and when it's not. Don't do like that, Timmie. . . . All right?"

Now she was really beginning to fear. Her voice was caught back. "Was I bad? Was I bad, Jan?"

"Yes. That was bad, Timmie."

Her throat was tight as a fist. "Ja-an . . ."

He relented. "No, you were just joking," he said.

"And wasn't I bad?"

"You were just kidding, Timmie," he said. "That's all right."

She breathed deep and then turned on her side and went happily to sleep. In a while Jan too was sleeping.

FIVE

AT THE END of a hard day she had been pushed too far. Her nerves were in shreds; she spoke in desperate exasperation. "Hake," she said, "it's *my* house."

"I knew it," he said. "I knew you was going to throw it up to me." He wagged his sallow head sagaciously. "I knew it was comin'. As long as I been here and as long as I been doing my part, I knew you was still going to throw it up to me. Ain't you took everything you could out of my pay check? Ain't I been working like a dog to help keep you and them two crazy young ones up? And now you go on and throw it up to me."

Her gaze flew to the photograph with the narrow brass

frame, propped on the maple china closet. Her large dark eyes met those flat unseeing eyes that she had tried so many thousands of times, in every minor tribulation, to read. But Robert's face didn't change; the round boyish face—softened lines that were already beginning to harden in Jan's face—still retained the gaily wistful smile that had so rarely been upon it when he was living. That December Sunday two years ago he had burned to death, bathed in a splash of fired gasoline, at Pearl Harbor. The face was saddening, the smile entirely indecipherable.

Uncle Hake knew where she was looking. "I know all about that too," he said, his voice an uncertain whine. "But I done said it was just the same as I did it. Him and me *was* going to go together to buy this house and property. We agreed on it. But it was just pure bad luck I couldn't keep my payments going. That trouble with my back." "Back trouble" was how Uncle Hake referred to the six months he had spent downstate in the Winton Sanitarium, drying out after a three-year drunk. "And then your husband Robert got called up, but it's easy for a man in the Army to save his money. That's the reason he could keep sending you the money back home, because Uncle Sam was paying his bed and board. And his clothes too. I've talked to lots of folks, good folks, about this very thing, and they said I was just as good as in on this property. Just a little bad luck at the beginning is all."

She passed her hand over her weary white face. "It's not the money, Hake. I don't care about the money or the house. . . ."

Again he wagged his head. "I'd like to know what else then, why you keep pestering me. You won't never give me a minute's peace."

"It's just that I've got to have more help, or more cooperation. . . ." She paused. Uncle Hake had deftly slipped off the greasy bedroom slipper and she thought for a moment that he was going to give her one of the weak slaps that he was always bestowing upon the children. But no, it was only a tiny gray spider marching alone over a white square of the linoleum.

Swat. "Damn spiders make my skin crawl," said Uncle Hake.

She spoke again, making sure that her voice stayed firm. "As I say, it's not the money. But I have to have more help, either from you or from someone else. I simply never get time to spend with the children any more, and with Robert gone, heaven knows they need me. They have to have someone. I really don't know at all what's to be done with Timmie. And I'm so tired when I come in, I'm afraid I'm too short with them sometimes."

Uncle Hake leaned back, tipping the front legs of his chair off the floor. He drummed the checkered tablecloth with his dark fingers. "Well, that's one thing you can't blame on me," he said. "I've told you, time and again I've told you, you was spoiling them two young ones. Letting them run around all day, doing just what they please and nothing else. They're like two wild things, and it's no wonder, if you ask me."

"Oh Hake. Be quiet a minute. My own brother, and I can't even talk to you."

He flinched slightly under her exasperated gaze. "Well, you're always pestering me," he said.

"The point is, I have to have more help, with the housework and with the children. I'm absolutely too tired to do a proper job after I get home." She worked as

32

a secretary to the shipping department manager of the paper mill, the same factory in which Uncle Hake worked. It was the principal—almost the only—industry near the small western North Carolina town. Their house on the six-acre farmlet was north of the town, not half a mile from the city limits.

"Well, Jenny," said Uncle Hake, "I guess I don't need you to tell me about being tired. I work like a dog, my God, I work just like a damn dog all the damn day in that lab. Old man Hickman gets crazier every day about how much work we got to do. 'Defense effort, we're part of the defense effort, boys. We got to do everything we can.' " He tried to imitate a deep growl with his high whiny voice. Mr. Hickman was Uncle Hake's foreman.

"What I want to know about, Hake, is whether you're willing to help pay for a maid. I absolutely have to have help and I'm going to get a girl at least part-time if I can."

"A maid? You want a maid for a six-room house? And with prices the way they are? Do you know what our expenses are? And a lot of them no use at all, as far as I can see. Did you know I wrote a twenty-four-dollar check today to the oil company, and that's on oil we've already burned up? Do you know that?"

She sighed weightily. "Yes, I know what the expenses are," she said. "And I know how prices are. I know as well as you do how we stand financially. I just wanted to know if you were willing to chip in on the salary for a maid."

"No, I can't do it."

She moved her chair slightly back from the table. "Well, that's all I wanted to know. I've got to have someone, and it would be a lot easier if you'd help. But if you won't, you won't. I hope I've got it figured how I can pay it alone. It means cutting down on the car payments and spreading them over a longer period of time, and I was hoping I wouldn't have to do that. But if you won't help, you won't help, and that's all there is to it."

She was giving him a clear easy way out and he was clearly going to take it, but first he would put up a pretense of justification. "It's not like that," he said, "it's not a bit like that, Jenny. I just can't afford it, I ain't got the money." He tipped the chair farther back, hooking his thumbs in the top of his dingy trousers. "Anyway," he said, and his voice held a queasy note of triumph, "anyway, it's a matter of principle."

"Principle?" She stared at him, a long square gaze with those dark eyes that brimmed with her forgiveness. Slowly, like a drop of oil soaking into a ball of cotton, a thin smile spread on her face. "All right then, Hake, all right." And into her clear warm voice had come an edge of sardonic amusement. She pushed the chair farther away and stood up. "I'd better go and check on the children," she said.

But by the time she was standing, before she had spoken, Jan was already gone from his hiding place by the door and with long silent strides had reached his bedroom door and eased it shut behind him, letting the knob silently over; and by the time the big rectangle of light entered the room through the door his mother had so quietly opened both he and Timmie were peacefully side by side in the two beds, he with his calm face toward the wall, away from the door and the mother.

Tenderly she closed the door and went back. Uncle Hake was already sitting in the flowery stuffed chair by the oil stove. Under the peach-colored light of the rickety floor lamp (that was another thing that needed fixing), he rattled the newspaper with more energy than he ever displayed in any other activity. She could tell by the way he sat, with the round shoulders slightly squared back into the chair, that he was pleased with himself for not giving in about the maid. She smiled, more fully than before. Poor Hake. It was so small and queer, the kind of thing that constituted dignity for him. "I ain't no family man," he had told her once. "I ain't no daddy." He had gone on to urge her to find a new husband, not realizing (poor Hake) that if she married again her brother would have to move, to find a new place to live.

In the little cramped dining room she began to gather the dishes, scraping the scraps into the garbage pail in the kitchen. She saw from Timmie's half-filled plate that the girl once again was not eating well. Jan's plate was of course cleaned, although the boy didn't actually eat: he merely chewed and swallowed whatever was on his plate, dutifully, as if he had been told to put more faggots on a fierce blazing bonfire. She piled the soiled dishes on the drainboard and leaned against the sink, waiting for the dishpan to fill. A little billow of steam rose from the sink and she breathed the moisture in deep, her eyes closed. She was weary to the marrow.

While she was drying the dishes and stacking them away in the shelves, she heard Uncle Hake rise from the deep chair—with a heartfelt groan—and slouch his way into his dull bedroom. He retired for the night—it was his way—without a good-night wish, and again she smiled. "Good night, Hake," she said to herself. Despite her tiredness she began to hum a tune, "My Blue Heaven," but broke off shortly the song that Robert used always to be whistling. She rubbed her dry cheek with her shoulder. She hoped that this night wouldn't be another night when she would wake with the metallic squeezed knot in the top of her throat, with the small tears running and running on her face.

She went into the living room and squared straight the few books on the tables, the cushions in the chairs, the flimsy doilies on the chair arms. She gathered and folded the newspaper that Uncle Hake had scattered, as a carrion-eater would scatter the inedible parts of a horse to get at the vitals. In the bedroom she unbuttoned herself from the cheap cotton dress and sat in her slip at the mirror. She examined her face: still not too bad, although the implacable loneliness was beginning to make itself visible in the tiny spiderweb above her cheekbones, directly under the big warm dark eyes. She raised her chin, looking, but there were no lines yet in the slender white neck. Except for her long black hair and the dark eyes she was fair all over, white; but this fairness was tinged, as if she sat by something immense and invisible which somehow still cast a warning shadow over her. Her image in the mirror was depressing, but still she looked, trying to learn. From her Jan had got his fair skin and his intensity, from Robert he had got his blondness and independence. The remainder, the remainder had not been passed to him on this earth. Timmie was all hers, a Nolan, with none of the blond Scandinavian Anderson blood.

Her eyes were melting with the small tears; they flocked on her cheeks like condensed moisture on an icy glass.

SIX

THE SCHOOLROOM was frenzied, seething, like an anthill under a constant dripping of boiling water. The children squirmed in the scratched bitter-tasting desks and peeped at each other. They whispered and murmured. On the second floor the window casements were high, and from their seats they could see nothing but immense depths of dirty gray sky, flat, as if the window-panes had been replaced with soiled paper. Jan sat in the row of desks near the window, looking at the initials carved into his desk, A.O.A., as if they made up a rune, a saying he could know and with which he could control his destiny. In the schoolroom the air flickered with missiles, tightly squeezed bits of paper; but only a few came near Jan, and these only by accident. The gang of all the children had long ago smelled the outsider in Jan, and they did not accept him. A flung spitball was a favor they conferred mutually upon one another, a sign of fraternity; for the outsider were reserved the twisted arm, the face ground into the cinders.

Today the uproar was over poetry. Someone had drawn on the blackboard in tall spidery letters which ran down at the ends of the lines:

JIMMY MARKOVICH IS
A SON OF A BICH.

Jimmy Markovitch now stood outside the door, silently whistling. Miz Harbison had said she wanted him out of the room to spare him embarrassment. With his mouth shut he whistled away; *his* feelings weren't hurt. He was waiting until Miz Harbison got back from the bathroom, where she had gone to have a talk, she said, with the other teachers. The teachers were always talking together in the bathroom.

When she came into the room again, the uproar disappeared, and a last single spitball sailed gently toward the back of the room. This Miz Harbison took care not to remark. She took her stand behind her small old scarred desk, a big square woman, gray all over, as if she had been constructed of soggy newsprint and left to harden. Her voice was opaque with authority, but brittle too, with secret veins of decay in it. She picked up a metal ruler and tapped the desk sharply. "I have decided," she said (*tick tick* with the ruler on the desk), "to allow the boy or girl who is guilty of that disgraceful writing on the blackboard to have a chance to report him or her self. It will go much easier on the guilty person if I hear from him. In a few minutes we will have our regular recess period, and I will be here at my desk and I hope to have that person come to see me. If I have to find out myself or if I hear it from another boy or girl, the punishment will be much harder, I can tell you." *Tick, tick, tick.* "Roy Burge, will you please take an eraser and erase that disgraceful writing which we are all ashamed to have such a thing in our nice classroom." She waited, tapping with the ruler, while a dark boy rubbed industriously at the lettering. "Don't believe for an instant that the guilty boy or girl will get away with it. That is absolutely untrue, I can tell you." The blackboard had been newly washed when the couplet was set down, and despite the boy's efforts the words were still visible, thin and ghostly, behind the gray smears of erasure. "And now we will all please open our geography books to page forty-four, to the map of India."

In a few minutes the recess bell rang and the classroom jolted into noise. *Whack.* Miz Harbison slapped the desk hard with the ruler. "Order, order," she said. "We must have order in all things. You must all file to the cloakroom now and you must get your wraps on quietly. And then we file quietly down the stairs. Isn't that right? And be sure you dress warmly."

At the outside door the students scattered like sparks from a Roman candle. They went running, shrill and suddenly red-faced. Jan poked along slowly by himself, a morose clenched person for whom recess was merely another part of the ordeal of school. Actually, recess was a partial respite now: Timmie was in one of her periods of fever and trembling. She lay at home in bed with her picture books and the stuffed giraffe while Mrs. Boggs, fat and chattering, ministered to her; so that Jan didn't have to stay with her on the school grounds to make sure that the tall sad girl—she was two full grades behind him now—wasn't tormented by the other children, who would find her and ring her about, baying like hounds. Timmie was home; Jan could seek his hiding place. He had found a way to get into the school furnace room without entering the front, to be stopped by the janitor. He could crawl in at the back, through a window which had been boarded up, but which had a loose frame. Inside there was not much room and he could go forward only a little way through the tangle of the big hot steam ducts. But he could get in and pull the window closed behind him, and there he was invisible even to the janitor, who was below in the fully dug basement, tending the furnace or dozing fitfully beside it. The only possible position he could take was to sit squatting on his heels, but this he learned to do without discomfort for long periods of time. Through a tiny peephole he could look directly into the booming murderous heart of the furnace. Red firelight leaped on his face, discovering the shadows and angles which would later appear there. In the fire he found interminable trains of imagery which, if interpreted correctly, offered him sacred information, celestial omens. He sat watching and listening without attention to the operation of his mind; it drummed steadily, like rain falling far across a valley.

After a while his time sense jarred him alert and he scuttled back through the web of wet ducts. The recess bell thrilled in the air as he closed back the window. Now the students poured muttering through the doors; it was no fun to go back. They filed into the room, into the cloakroom, and then came back to their seats. Miz Harbison was at her desk, and they seated themselves quietly. She stood in her place, tapping patiently with the ruler until they were still.

"Jan Anderson," she said, "I want to talk to you out in the hall. And I don't want to hear any noise from the rest of you." She waited while he looked at her, completely puzzled. "Come along," she told him. Holding herself stiff, she marched through the door.

Jan came slowly after. He hated the sensation of all those eyes upon him.

When he came through the door she was already bent over to look him square in the face. He returned her look flatly and she blinked her gray eyes quickly three, four times. But her voice was steady, thick. "I understand that you're responsible for that disgraceful writing on the blackboard this morning," she said. "It would have been much better if you had told me yourself."

"Not me," he said. "I didn't write nothing."

She blinked again. "Anything," she said, "I didn't write anything." She put her hand to her gray corded throat. "I happen to know that you did, young man. It only makes it worse when you tell a story about it."

"It wasn't me."

"Keep quiet. I don't remember when I've met a boy so obstinate. You're just getting yourself in deeper and deeper."

"Not me," he said. "I never wrote nothing." He kept those blunt eyes forcibly on her own.

Her gray face began to tinge pink, perhaps from bending to him. "Anything," she said again. "I've never written anything." She stood straight and looked down at him with sharp disgust. "I've never met so obstinate a child, never. Well, this is out of my hands now. You must report to the principal; he'll talk to you and then we'll see. Do you know where the principal's office is?"

Jan nodded.

"Well then, go along. He wants to talk to you."

Jan gave her the hard baffled look, not moving.

"Go along now, I said. Do you want me to lead you there by your ear?"

He went, going slowly, keeping to the right wall. The halls were silent, but when he passed classroom doors he heard the industrious buzz and twitter of education—all of it meaningless to him. The building smelled of oiled floors, of chalk dust, of the sourness of excited bodies and the mushroomy odor of wet rubber galoshes and wet wool. He went slowly down the stairs, considering the simplest and easiest way to act. From the silvery radiators stationed at intervals along the lower hall came the soft belch of heating water.

The principal's office was in the other of the two school buildings, and he crossed the small cemented square between them hunched over, his fists tight in his pockets. The sky had got darker and he felt cold tiny specks of rain on the back of his neck. He entered the west building and climbed another flight of stairs.

In the principal's office he had to wait. The young knife-faced lady told him to sit, Mr. Guthrie would see him in a moment. He let his legs dangle from the tough oak bench and watched her as she bent over the type-writer, scrubbing at the sheet of paper with an eraser. She sat forward and leaned to blow away the fragments of rubber, her cheeks puffed, her bright brown hair falling forward over her face. For all her sharpness of feature and voice she was pretty. He watched her constantly and she glanced at him once with a nettled expression. She looked as if she were going to speak to him and then had decided not to.

The oak door to the principal's chamber opened and a young man nodded his way out. He carried a stuffed briefcase and he said, "Well, we'll get together on it after the first of the month, then." He came in and began to talk to the girl at the typewriter, but she cut him short. "All right," she said to Jan, "you go on in now."

He went in and again stood waiting, his hands in his pockets. The principal was writing on a pad of pink paper and Jan watched his dark shiny bald head with the sparse hairs streaked back over it like pencil marks. Finally he looked up at Jan, his dark face firm and serious. "Oh yes," he said. "You're the boy that was sent to me, aren't you?"

Jan nodded.

"Take your hands out of your pockets," he said. "Stand up straight."

He did this.

"Now, you know that what you did is a very serious thing, don't you? That's not the kind of thing a boy of your age does if he's going to be any account. You understand that?"

He nodded.

"Don't shake your head like something dumb. Answer when you're spoken to."

"All right."

He slapped the glass desk top with his big hairy hand. "And not like that. You say Yes sir. Yes sir—that's the way you show respect to someone. Do you understand?"

"Yes sir."

"Now what you did is a very serious thing; it's the

kind of thing that hoodlums and hardened criminals start out by doing. You don't want to be a criminal, a gangster, do you?"

"No sir."

"Do you know what happens to criminals and gangsters? They get put in jail and they don't ever get to come out. Nobody gets to come and see them; not even their mothers can visit them. They lock them up away from everybody else and feed them on bread and water. How do you think you'd like that, to be locked up and have nothing to eat but bread and water?"

He said nothing.

"Would you like that?"

"No sir."

"But that's just where you're headed if you don't watch your conduct. Now I think I know what your mother would say if she knew you'd done something like that. She'd give you a good talking-to, wouldn't she?"

"Yes sir."

"She might even bend you over her knee and warm your britches for you, isn't that right?"

"Yes sir."

He leaned back in the swivel chair, laying his palms flat on the desk. "Now this is the first time you've ever been in my office, I think. Is that right?"

"Yes sir."

"Well—" He stopped and peered with puzzled eyes into Jan's face. "Is something wrong with your eyes?" he asked.

"What?"

"What's wrong with your eyes?"

"Nothing, I guess."

"Sir."

44

"Sir."

"What are you looking at me like that for? It's rude to stare at people that way. Don't you know that?"

"Yes sir."

"Well, seeing as how this is your first time in here, I'm not going to punish you much," he said. "I just want you to remember what I've told you and for you to think about it. I want you to take what I've told you to heart. Think it over. Do you understand?"

"Yes sir."

"And I don't want to see you back in here any more. If you're sent to me again it's going to go a lot harder on you. Next time you'll be in real trouble and it'll have to go a lot harder. Is that clear?"

"Yes sir."

He leaned forward again and picked up a printed form; laid it down and took a mechanical pencil from his breast pocket; screwed a lead tip out into sight. "Well, you clear out and get back to class. You've already missed too much; you might have missed something already it would be important for you to know in later life. And I don't want to see you in here any more. Good-bye now."

"Yes sir." Jan went out.

In the outer office the man with the briefcase was talking in a quick earnest voice to the lady at the typewriter. The briefcase was sitting on the floor, and he was perched on the low wooden railing with one foot propped on the heavy case. He wore thin bright blue socks. She gave him her rapt attention and a full but wary smile. But when Jan entered she watched him all the way out. When he turned at the door she gave a small involuntary shiver.

He went back to his classroom. Outside the door he

paused, deliberating, rather pleased with himself on the success of his determined acting. He went in. All the faces looked up at him, white fervid flowers under a soft rain. He raked them over with the blunt blue gaze as they returned his stare curiously. Only one boy, Ronny Hughes—who was called "Root," for some forgotten reason—did not look at Jan, but kept his head down and peeped up, obviously hoping to remain unnoticed. . . . So he had discovered what he needed to, and, looking at the floor in order not to give it away, he crossed the room and took his seat. With his finger he traced the carved A.O.A. on the desk.

Miz Harbison said, "Jan, this is our arithmetic lesson now. You will please open your arithmetic workbook to Exercise Seventeen."

SEVEN

IMMIE LAY hushed and expectant, squeezed over to the far edge of the little bed. A thin film of sweat lay on her forehead and her face was bright, feverish, almost incandescent. He lay beside her, propped high on the pillows, and as he read he moved his finger beneath the words so that she could see them plainly. He filled his voice with sincere interest: "Once upon a time there were four little Rabbits, and their names were—Flopsy, Mopsy, Cotton-tail, and Peter."

She was looking at the picture. "Which one is that?" She placed a clear finger on a rabbit's head. "And which one is that? Is that Mother Rabbit?"

Jan read on. "Peter was most dreadfully frightened; he rushed all over the garden, for he had forgotten the way back to the gate."

"Who's that?" she asked, pointing.

"That's Mr. McGregor."

"What's that he's got? Is it a rake he's got?"

"No, it's just a big long comb."

"Will he hurt Peter?"

"No, he's only going to comb his hair, to make it pretty." He cleared his throat. "Mr. McGregor was quite sure that Peter was somewhere in the toolshed, perhaps hidden underneath a flower-pot. He began to turn them over carefully, looking under each."

"Is Mr. McGregor bad, Jan?"

"No, he's not bad, he's only joking."

"Is he just kidding?"

"Yes, he's kidding, he's pretending." He stroked her long hair smooth. "I am sorry to say that Peter was not very well during the evening. . . . But Flopsy, Mopsy, and Cotton-tail had bread and milk and blackberries for supper."

She hunched closer to him and put her head on his left arm. "Bread and milk and blackberries," she said. "That's real good for supper. That's good, isn't it?"

"It's a lot better than just bread and water," he said. He smiled and patted her shoulder.

"Read another story."

"No, that's enough for right now. I'll read you another one after a while."

"Will you read about the Owl and the Pussycat?"

"Yes, I'll read that."

"Jan, Jan," she said. She was excited. "What happens when it gets dark?"

"The sun goes away."

"Who takes it away?"

"Nobody takes it, it just goes away by itself."

"Where does it go?"

He pointed west. "It goes over there behind the hills, and then it lies down and goes to sleep."

"Like I do?"

"Just like you do. It finds a place down in between the hills and goes to sleep. It looks like a big red lake when it lies down."

"How did it get up in the sky?"

"The Indians got it to go up in the sky to keep them warm. They were cold because there wasn't any sun in the sky. So they made a real big round fat man out of straw; he was as big as this house, bigger than the house. Then they covered him all over with tar; it was a kind of tar that would burn real bright and never burn out, and they got the wise man to come and make him alive. As soon as he was alive the big fat man that was straw started sayin' I'm cold, I'm cold, oh it's cold down here, I'm cold. And the wise man said, Yes this is a cold place all right, but we can help you out; I'll tell you what to do. And then they took the big fat straw man over to this great big balloon they had built and put him in it. And the wise man said, Now this balloon will take you way up in the sky and when it stops you get out and take this here match and strike it and put it on your toe and then you will be warm. And then the straw man got in the balloon and went up and set fire to his foot with the match. Then he started burning all over and he jumped up and said, Oh I'm warm, I'm really warm. It made him real happy, but he had to stay up in the sky because nobody could get near him, he was so hot."

49

"Were the Indians glad then?"

"Yes, they were glad because they had made them a sun that would keep them warm and they could see by it."

"Did it hurt the big fat straw man to be burned on fire?"

"No, no. It just got him warm; he was real happy about it."

"Would it hurt me to get burned?"

"Yes, it would hurt Timmie to get burned."

"I won't get burned then," she said firmly.

"Good. That's right," he said. He rose from the bed. "I'll be back in a little while."

She held the stuffed animal up. "Say good-bye to him first."

He patted the stuffed head which had long ago lost all its coloring. "Good-bye, Ralph Giraffe," Jan said. He went through the door.

She closed her eyes, watching with her mind the brilliant polychrome specks and shapes that danced and metamorphosed behind her eyelids. She wriggled toward the middle of the bed; where Jan had lain it was warm and damp. When he had got up his shirt behind had a single long streak of wet, the shape of a big icicle. She too was damp, but she didn't mind.

Outside it was raining. Small streaklets came down softly; it was like a weighty mist. She listened to it pittering on the window sill like a conversation among small dry unimaginable insects. She opened her eyes. The small rain was gray, falling on the oak tree and the lawn and making them cool. The white curtains with the red and yellow spots were motionless; then they stirred, bellying slightly outward toward the gray rain.

She raised the clammy sheet and maneuvered Jannie

under. She got the long colorless neck between her legs and hugged it there tightly. The muscles of her thighs were clenched. She closed her eyes again. The rain smelled cool and earthy, and with her eyes closed it sounded louder and nearer; it seemed to be in the room, falling small and touchless upon her; it was clear, intemerate as the sky. She opened her eyes and the rainy room darted through the window of the unraining room, and outside it expanded, to fill the whole world with the gray veil of droplets. She thought that it need never stop.

What if she and Jan and the mother ran away? What if they left the house and Uncle Hake and lived in a cave in the woods? They would build fires and sleep in blankets on the floor of the cool cave and watch the rain fall hard outside. Big green leaves would fill with water and cup it so that when the rain was gone they could go outside and sip the water from the leaves. Jan would make the fluffy pink birds that had careful eyes like his talk to her; they would tell her all about the forest, how the Indians had built it so that they would have a place to hide. Jan would gather huge sweet blackberries, and Mrs. Boggs would follow the path from this house, bringing milk and bread to them. At night they would build a fire and Jan would tell her and the mother stories.

The rain was harder now, and she could see that the drops were larger. The air had got whiter with the rain and the big oak tree was dim behind it and seemed far distant. With her thighs she squeezed Jannie's neck rhythmically and nuzzled its head into her belly. She pinched her eyes tight and opened them again. The rain made a thin drumming sound on the smooth lawn and it had begun to come inward upon the window sill. The spotted curtains drifted carefully toward her.

And then the mother would die, there would be nothing but a big pile of bones, and she and Jan and Jannie would be together in the cave. The sunlight would fall through the forest leaves in pretty pieces on the ground. Jan would teach her everything he knew; it would take a long time, days and days. He would sit across from her, perched on his heels in the shadowy cool cave, and talk and talk. She would understand it all, his voice warm and steady, his warm eyes full on hers. She would care for Jannie, and Jan would bring in the great juicy blackberries, mounded in the pail so high they would brush his knuckles as he swung them along under the high trees. He would go firmly through the forest always looking about himself, looking at everything. Across the spangled glade she would see him coming steadily to the cave. The sunlight would lie in his hair like yellow silk.

It was coming down harder. The sky had got black and massive, and the raindrops were big and far apart. The wind was bigger too, and was tall and breathy in the room, carrying the curtains inward behind it like long flapping coattails. The thunder uttered guttural belches. The sky became suddenly livid, and after the lightning the ponderous air smacked together with a sound like a tree felled. In the bedroom it was cooler now, but her body had got hotter. Her temples were running with bitter sweat and she wiped it away with the back of her wrist. Her skin was soft and sticky like oily cotton. Her thighs narrowed, she pumped at the stuffed long neck; it too was wet and hot.

The forest would always be cool, even the silky yellow sunlight would be cool. The paths would be wide and gentle. The trees would be straight. All the greenery would be deep and gentle. When the horizon was intemperate, when the sky gasped and staggered with the storms, Jan would keep her close. He would stroke her hair smooth and tell her all the warm calm things. His hand would lie on her hair, on her neck, moving only slightly, unbelievably gentle. He sat hunkered on his heels as she nestled to him, and she pressed his assured hand to her belly and clutched it there while the storm got worse, the rain falling in throbbing floods. It came down harder and harder and the sky was black as asphalt until suddenly it was instantly white all over with a leviathanic spasm of electricity. The immense vistas of her wishing snapped closed and for a moment she was blinded by the simultaneity of her loss and gain. She gagged for breath, her face was melting with sweat, her eyes were choked with exhausting tears. The boom of the thunderclap made the whole house quiver. "Let's . . . don't leave the . . . cave," she said. She was gagging and sobbing.

Then she lay still, totally soaked with sweat. Outside it rained hard, but it was steady now and not wild, and already she could sense the slacking of it. Her soft body was heaving for breath. Between her thighs it was burning with a sticky film, like her mouth after one of the desiccating fever dreams. She turned on her side with Jannie still tight to her, and with an edge of the sheet she mopped at her face. Her hair too was wet. At last her bones stopped shivering. She closed her eyes, and, to the sound of the rain growing softer, she fell into a level doze which was immediately filled with large fluffy pink birds, each having Jan's kind eyes instead of the mean glassy bird eyes. They did not really fly, but floated about like balloons, and they were not really real birds because in some way they were responsive to her desires, her fears. Soon the birds had turned into big pink clouds which were at first pleasantly motionless. The clouds pulled apart like thin cloth to show a bright blue sky, empty but for a speck far in the background. Her dream eyes fought to look at this mote, and it began to enlarge, to come forward. She saw that it was a hand with its merciful palm turned toward her. It was a beautiful hand, white, smooth as wax. In the center of the palm was a bit of glass, darkly red, dark as blood. She sighed in her sleep.

The rain had stopped. A pale glimmer of sunlight played on the smooth wet lawn; in the sky the storm was dismembering itself.

EIGHT

M<small>RS. BOGGS</small> was the woman the mother had got to help with the housework and sometimes to take care of the children, especially Timmie, if she was ill and couldn't go to school. It was obvious from the first that this big fine lady wasn't going to work at the Anderson house for many months; it was Uncle Hake, of course. The first moment he saw her he began to bitch: "My God, Jenny, I don't see how you expect a woman like that to keep up a house. My God, she can't even keep herself up. Did you ever see anybody so fat and sloppy? Just look at her. My God." Of course, Mrs. Boggs had horse sense; she saw in an instant what Uncle Hake was, and she decided that she wasn't going to pay any mind to *his* lip. But it was never so simple with Uncle Hake: he was always there unchanging; like a big mind-rat he gnawed at the nerves.

Often Mrs. Boggs would stop for a moment and sit in a chair beside the mother and take those pale hands in her own big ham-colored hands and say, "Lord, Miz Anderson, nobody knows what troubles you've got. That brother of yours, I declare . . ." She nodded her clumsy face sadly. The mother smiled and murmured, "Oh no, not at all." But she was actually pleased and she fluttered her pretty dark eyelashes as if she were being courted by a handsome new beau. Around this time there was something scary about the mother: shadows were gathering about her eyes and under the lines of her jaw; she looked as if she had gone all hollow inside.

For all her fumbling and her heavy body—she could be felt moving about anywhere in the house because of the jarring floor—the big red lady was efficient. The house was got shiny inside, and it was easy to wonder if Jan wasn't looking at everything around him now for the new pleasure of it. The place stayed in order. Somehow she had got her heavy rambles scheduled so that she could straighten up the messes Uncle Hake was always making. She kept the disheveled newspapers cleared and the subtle cigar ashes swept up, and maybe this order contributed to his orneriness.

She treated the family as she felt she ought to. Timmie's fear of her was not inordinate; after a while she accepted the coarse woman and didn't hide. Mrs. Boggs was gentle, tried to treat the girl easily, but that body and that temperament simply did not allow gentleness to leak through: it came out as a half-subdued loud joviality.

And for Timmie she was always just another bigger, less troubling, more mobile Uncle Hake. Naturally, Jan puzzled her completely. She would come upon him laboring over some contraption—he was always making strange little devices of some kind—and she would clap him on the back hard and comradely, leaving for a few seconds the white imprint of her big hand under his shirt. "You're a queer young fellow, you know it?" she said. "You're really a *quair* young man."

"Mnghnm," Jan said.

"Really a queer boy. What are you making there?"

"Nothing."

"Eh? Well, I hope it works, then."

He looked up at her and smiled faintly. She gave him a grin like a sword slash.

Uncle Hake gave her hell. He shook his round little fist in her face, and it seemed that if she had wanted to she could have leaned over and bitten it off and swallowed it at one gulp. "You keep the hell out of my room," he said. It was a whine. "You damn old fat biddy. I don't want you nosing around in my things all the time. My God, can't a man have any privacy? Can't I have a minute of peace and quiet?"

"You old goat," she said. Her voice was louder and deeper than his. "You ought to be ashamed," she said, "picking on these nice kids, driving your poor sister half out of her mind. If it was my place . . ." She nodded her head sadly.

"It ain't your goddam place. I wish you'd find where your goddam place is, one time. I wish you'd learn to keep your nose where it belongs."

"For my part, I don't care." She was becoming calmer and steadier, while Uncle Hake was getting more and more excited. "You can live like a pig. I'm trying to keep a clean house, and that room is an eyesore; it ruins the rest of my work. But if you want to live like a hog . . ."

"I'll live like I want; it ain't none of your goddam business how I live. Talk about hogs. Whoever saw such a fat old sow. Just keep the goddam hell out of my room, that's all. My God, a man works like a dog all the damn day long and in this crazy house he don't get nothing but bother, not a minute's peace do I get."

"You old goat," she said, "I know you. You're just afraid I'll see something in that room you don't want people to know you've got."

This infuriated him to the limit. He was as jerky as a puppet. His voice had got higher in pitch, he spoke in a mean squeaky treble. "You goddam old bitch. If they was as many sticking out of you as they's been stuck in you, you'd look like a porkypine."

For answer she grasped him by the shoulder and by the top of his greasy trousers and flung him tumbling across the room against the wall. He landed with a plop like a bag of wet laundry. He glared at her with his yellowed eyes, feeling his body to see if it was still stuck together. She wasn't even breathing hard, and she turned her back on him and marched away, gathering to her ludicrous body as much dignity as she could muster. She didn't give him a backward glance. He got up, still feeling his mortified flesh, and, without saying anything, went into his room. They heard him blundering around, choking out curses, and then he came out. He went straight outside and they watched him maneuvering around in the lawn, kicking at the grass. In his mouth was an unlighted cigar. He ground it between his dingy teeth until it was nothing but a mushy frazzle.

Mrs. Boggs had gone straight to the mother to apologize. "If you want to send me packing, that's all right," she said. "I can sure understand how you'd want to; I didn't have no call to lose my temper like that. You'd be within your rights to give me notice."

"Oh no, oh no," she murmured. "Hake is difficult. I'm sure it was as much his fault as anyone's."

Mrs. Boggs nodded her square red face. "I declare— that man . . ."

Then the mother's face was filled with the small tears, and her throat clucked with gentle half-caught sobs. She put her lovely ivory-colored face into Mrs. Boggs's shoulder. The big woman patted her roughly on the back and put her other arm around the mother's thin waist. "Honey, that's all right, I know how you feel. Lord, I could tell you things. . . ." Her solid face made a slight movement of surprise. "Lord, honey, you've got to start eating something. You're skinny as a rake, I swear it. You've got to put some meat on them poor bones." This only caused the mother to sob more wildly and to begin to weep in little murmurs. "Oh Lord, honey, oh Lord . . ." said Mrs. Boggs. She took a big blue bandanna from her apron pocket and wiped at the mother's face.

She would find Jan poking about somewhere and say to him: "You're sure a quiet-enough young man. But what do you do around here all day long?"

"Nothing."

"Nothing, eh? Well, why don't you do what you want to, then? Why don't you go off and find the other boys around here? Maybe they could show you how to play ball or something, eh?"

Jan said nothing.

"My Lord, honey, don't look at me like that," she said. "I could swear you was going to bite my heart out." She would go on dusting or sweeping, nodding her head, bewildered.

She would come into Timmie's room and look fondly on the big soft girl in the bed. "Hello, sweetheart, how are you doing?"

Timmie nodded.

"Well, sweetie, do you want me to read you a story?"

"Not right now," she said, not being able to imagine the huge lady beside her on the feverish bed.

"Well, if you want anything you just come and tell me, just tell Miz Boggs. Eh?"

She too would not answer.

Momentarily discouraged, Mrs. Boggs would shake her head sadly. "Well now, you remember what I told you, sweetheart." And she would go away with all her hearty affections dampened. It was a queer tight-lipped house. Except for Uncle Hake, of course.

It was all too clear that she couldn't stay on much longer. Her good nature had been too often rebuffed, even though this had happened sometimes more or less accidentally. She had no really reliable allies against Uncle Hake: the mother was too soft, the children too . . . what? "Shut up in themselves," she would say. One day she told the mother she couldn't stay on any longer, it was working on her mind too grim. The mother agreed, nodding dumbly.

"I hate to leave you like this," she said. "I feel like I'm leaving you with a worse mess than before I got here. But I really got to look after myself some too, honey. Vance—he's my middle boy—he's just like a wild dog; he ain't learned no respect, no nothing. If it wasn't for the war and him maybe getting shot or killed, I swear I'd be glad for him to go in the Army. I swear he'd be a lot better off, my mind'd be a lot more at ease. But Lord knows you got troubles enough without mine." She took the blue bandanna from her pocket; it was knotted tightly. "I wanted to give you these before I left. So you'd remember me, when I was with you." She untied the knot and showed the two pearl earrings lying in the cloth like white eyes. "I found these up home the other day when I was cleaning out some old drawers. I don't know where they come from, must of been somebody in Jim's family—he was my first husband. Anyway, they're so little and p'tite. You're the only one I know could wear them." She went from the house for the last time; the mother still held the earrings open in her hand.

Uncle Hake had kept to his room all that day, but now he came out sniggering. He was as happy as a cow. Jan watched his uncle watching Mrs. Boggs lumber away. Beneath the tangled blond brow his face was sour, musingly troubled.

NINE

H<small>E SPOTTED</small> Root Hughes alone for the moment across the school playground, and started toward him, keeping out of his line of vision. The idea was to let himself be discovered, and this he managed by going obliquely and getting behind the tall red-faced boy and then dropping the cylinder so that it rang on the cement walk. It was a brass cylinder, four inches long and two inches in diameter, with a cap that screwed on one end. It was smooth, shiny, pleasantly hefty in the hand. He stooped immediately to get it when he dropped it and stuffed it into the pocket of his corduroys with obvious haste. A shiny round end was visible at the mouth of his pocket. He was satisfied. But Hughes was already looking over his shoulder.

"What's 'at thing?" Root Hughes asked. His voice was thin and grating.

"What's what thing?" said Jan.

"This right here."

The taller boy's hand darted for his pocket, but Jan was too quick for him. With his own hand he clapped the cylinder hard against his thigh and spun around to face the other. "Nothing," said Jan.

"Yes it is. I saw it."

"It ain't nothing."

"Yes it is. I can see it in your pocket."

"It ain't nothing."

He held his hand out. "Let me see it."

Jan kept his eyes carefully down, centered on the base of Root's throat. "Better not," he said.

"Better not, chicken squat. How come you better not?"

"I better not."

"I seen it, it's a round long hickey. I already seen what it is."

"Well," said Jan.

"So let me see it again. It ain't no secret to me now."

"Better not."

"Oh manoo-oor. Give me that hickey. I'll give it right back."

Jan looked secretively about himself. No one was watching them. "I'll let you see part of it, but don't tell nobody." He lipped the pocket back, exposing about half the cylinder. He made certain Root saw the brass cap screwed on.

The other boy snatched at it, but Jan danced back, slapping his hand over the pocket.

63

"Oh manure, let me see it. Give it right back, swear I will." He held up his left hand, palm out. "I swear on my mother's bones," he intoned.

Jan still seemed fearful. He scraped a figure on the wet walk with the toe of his tennis shoe. "I could let you see it, maybe, but you got to swear you won't tell nobody."

"I won't tell nobody."

"You got to swear, though."

He raised the hand again. "I swear on my mother's bones."

Jan produced it and held it up for an instant, looking all about at the other kids. He put it back into his pocket.

"Oh duck squat," Root said. "Let me *see* it. Let me have it in my hand a minute. Give it right back, cross my heart."

A few minutes before the recess bell rang Jan finally gave it over. Root turned it over and over and about in his hands; hefted it. "It's sort of heavy," he said. He began to unscrew the cap.

Jan, standing close, snatched it back. "That's enough," he said.

Root looked at him ruefully. "What's inside of it?"

"Nothing."

"Yes there is, or you wouldn't do like that. What's it got in it?"

"Nothing."

"Don't gimme that stuff. There's something in it or you wouldn't act like that."

"You got to promise not to tell. . . . Anyway, I better not say."

With Sisyphean persistence Root gouged it out of him.

64

In the shiny cylinder was a big white furry spider with three big eyes. "I found it in the barn," Jan said. "I ain't never seen nothing like it around here before." It had been awful hard to catch, could run like a flash. Jan couldn't open the cylinder: what if it got away? You couldn't catch it in a month of Sundays. He thought maybe it was going to have babies too. Really was a crazy-looking thing, big as three of your fingers. No, he didn't think it would bite you and kill you; hadn't got no mouth, at least, he hadn't seen no mouth. ? ? Maybe it ate with its legs, sucked things up like through straws. He was going to look at it when he got home, and see. No. Absolutely could not open it up here. It got away, you'd never catch it. Think of the trouble with Miz Harbison and the principal, all of the teachers.

They agreed to meet after school. Root would go over to Jan's house with him. In Jan's barn there was a big box: you could get down inside and look at it and it couldn't get away. Solemn injunction not to tell anybody; solemn response, endangering the maternal bones. Okay then; it was agreed.

The day was overcast and in the filthy light the boys' bodies looked dark and gaunt. A lousy flock they were, sniffling and snuffling and shuffling. In their clothes they were smeared and steamy, and they talked together without surcease and without sense. The bell ending recess drilled the dank air, and they hurried together at the schoolhouse door like insects ganging to dispense with a morsel of decayed meat. They were all sour with fear, egoism, frustration.

At the end of the school day they met in the cloakroom. Both fought wordlessly to get into the slick rubber raincoats and the overshoes. When they got outside, it had begun to drab down spitlets of rain, and they slogged over the muddy sucking roads the two miles to Jan's house. He kept a careful distance from Root, figuring correctly that the taller boy would attempt to overpower him and take away the hickey. All the way home there was enough room between them for Jan to have a comfortable running head start, though they talked together amiably enough.

They went straight to the barn. He had brought them around on the road that ran above the field of sagegrass, not wanting anyone in the house to know they had arrived. They entered the small abandoned barn and Jan closed the big loose doors behind them and dropped the crossbar into the slots. "There," he said. "Can't nobody bother us now." He unsnapped his raincoat and took it off and flopped it over the low wall of a horse stall. "Whoo," he said. "That thing's hot."

Root obediently removed his slicker and put it beside Jan's. He rubbed his red face. "All right," he said, "let's see that hickey. I don't believe there's no spider in there. Footsy Pavlat said there wasn't no such of a thing as a spider like that."

Jan eyed him levelly, directly now. "I thought you wasn't going to tell nobody," he said.

"Well, I didn't. I just ast him if he ever seen any spiders like you said."

"I bet you did tell him too. I bet you told him I had it."

"I never."

"I bet you did."

"Well, so what if I did? You ain't got no spider that's big and white and's got three eyes, neither."

"You might could've seen whether I did or not if you hadn't of told Footsy Pavlat."

"Well, chicken squat. Give me that hickey and I'll see if there's any spider."

"Not now I ain't, after you told Footsy Pavlat."

They went through the whole ritual again. Root Hughes would have just taken it from Jan—he was undoubtedly the stronger—but he was leery of the other boy here on his own territory; the house wasn't too far away, and no telling who he might conjure up with a yell or so. Besides, in the dim light in the barn, Jan's big blunt eyes looked meaner, businesslike; he kept turning them on Root like sharp sticks jabbed at him. Finally Jan agreed to allow him, under certain conditions, to look. He led him through a creaky gate into a disused horse stall. It smelled sweetly of dung long desiccated and of the falling rain. He showed him the box he would have to get into: it had been a large hay trough for the horse. The small grain box that had been above it had been removed, and a tripartite board cover had been hinged to the top of the trough. All this handiwork was Jan's, of course. The trough itself had been freshly partitioned with two thin sheets of plywood; the center space was much larger than the section on either side, large enough to accommodate Root's hunched body, although very uncomfortably.

Jan nodded at it. "You'll have to get down in there first. Then I can hold down the lid so it can't get away." The lids for the two side sections were down; the lid for the middle section was up, latched back to the frame of the stall.

Root hesitated, hearing the small rain sprinkle on the low tin roof above. He shook his head. "It ain't big enough," he said. "I ain't about to get in that box." He stepped back.

67

"Well," Jan said placidly. He turned away.

Root had come along too far not to go through with it; stepped forward again; peered inside. He lifted the lids of the other two sections. They were empty. "It's too damn little," he said.

"Have to scrunch down. I ain't going to let this thing get away."

Root meditated. "If I get down in this box and open that hickey and you're telling me a big lie, will you bend over and let me kick your ass?"

Jan didn't waver. "All right. If I ain't telling the truth," he said.

This surrender mollified the red-faced boy in large measure. After more disputation he finally straddled the side of the stall and got inside. He wriggled about, trying to find an unawkward position. "I told you it ain't big enough," he said.

"Don't have to be so big. You ain't going to be in there but just long enough to see it. You got to promise to help me catch it back, though."

"Well." His voice sounded queer and hollow inside the box.

Jan unlatched the lid and held it up with his left hand; with the other he produced the bright brass cylinder from his pocket and gave it to Root. "Here," he said. "Now don't open it till I get the lid down. It'll get away, sure as I'm telling you." He dropped the lid and fitted the latch plate over the hasp.

"Wait a minute. I can't see nothing in here, it's so black."

"That spider's white," Jan said. "It'll shine in the dark." He slipped the smooth whittled peg into the hasp, found a length of wood and drove the peg tight.

Root was excited; then exasperated. "I've got this damn hickey open," he said, "and there ain't nothing in it. I knew there wasn't going to be no spiders. Let me out of here because I get to kick your ass."

Jan turned and pulled himself up to sit squarely on the lid. With his thumb he checked the peg; it was tight as a nail. Through the wood he felt Root heave upward under his thighs.

"Let me out of here, goddam you. Just for this I get to kick your ass three times."

"All right."

The noise in the box subsided. Then Root said, "Let me out, Jan. My legs is busting, scrunched up like this."

He drummed his soft heels lightly on the side of the trough. "You know why they wasn't no spider in that tube? Because I didn't put him in, that's why. I was telling you a lie that it didn't bite. It has three big teeth right in front, just like a big rattlesnake's teeth, except bigger. If it was to bite you, you'd swell up like a big balloon and just turn black. You'd die dead as a doornail. It'd bite you in a minute, down there in the box. You'd be a dead man right this minute."

The other yelled as loud as he could, and Jan felt the boards resonate slightly. Even here next to the box the yell didn't sound very loud, but he wished the rain would come down harder. That would drown it out sure. "Can't nobody hear you," he said in a lazy dreamy voice.

"You shitass. I'm going to kick the piss out of you. And I don't believe that duck squat about no spider neither."

"Keep telling you you don't want to see this here spider, but you won't believe me," Jan said. He dropped gently off the top of the box and went over to a corner of the stall. He raked back dull old straw and pieces of

69

rotten burlap to uncover four crude cages. They were filled with nervous gray mice; by now he had collected scores of them. He brought two cages back to the trough.

Root was still talking. ". . . your ass. Let me out of here, my legs is busting."

"But there is too a spider like I said," Jan said firmly. He knocked on the lid of the partition on the left side. "Listen. I'm going to put him down in here. He can't get to you, so you don't need to worry. He can't get to you unless I raise up that wall on this side. I bet you didn't know I could raise that wall up." He picked up a cage and selected one of the largest mice; plucked it out by a delicate pink ear. He opened the lid and dropped the mouse in; it skittered about on the smooth bottom of the trough.

Root recoiled violently in the box. He was silent for long moments. Then he said, "Let me out of here, you shitass. That ain't no spider, that's you scrabbling your hand around down in there. That don't even sound like a spider."

Not bothering to answer, Jan took from his back pocket a largish crumb of soda cracker and placed it in the trough against the base of the plywood partition. The mouse scurried to it, bright-eyed, noisy; it brushed its hairy back against the wall. "That ain't my hand," Jan said. "I bet you can tell that. That ain't me."

"Don't you raise that wall up," Root said. He breathed heavily between his words.

"Well. I don't know. You lucky you ain't already been bit by one of them things. I guess this is the only place in the world where there's spiders like this, big and white like that, with them three eyes and them three big long teeth. You ain't been looking out for them at all

70

because I been watching you. You're just lucky, is all, that you ain't been bit and swole up and be dead. Turn black as tar. Around here you got to be looking out for them all the time. They're fast as a rabbit to come at you and bite you."

"That's just a lot of manure. Let me out. My back is hurting me."

"Me, I just catch these old spiders," said Jan. "Just wear me some big railroad gloves and when they come after me I just grab them and put them in a sack. I got a whole lot of them. Boy, you ought to seen what they done to that big old dog that was around here. He swole up like a big balloon. I guess I got a hundred spiders like that saved up."

Root Hughes started bawling. He let out long-drawn howls as if he were singing some wild unintelligible song. He kept saying Jan was a shitass and telling him to let him out.

Jan regarded the noisy box speculatively. He went to the door of the stall, reached to the ledge and took down two pieces of cooked chicken, rancid and greasy. He opened the lid to the other partition and placed the two slick bits of flesh at the base of each plywood wall. The other boy was still crying, but not so loudly now. Then he got the other two cages and dumped them in the right partition. The two that were already before the trough he dumped into the left. The mice flurried crazily to the meat.

Keek. Keerk, keerk, keek. Keek.

The central box was loud with shrieks and weeping. Root Hughes kept trying to get the curses completely uttered; he really was quite hysterical. With a long stick Jan was keeping the mice lively; stirred them round and

71

round, as if he were churning buttermilk. They were crazy for the chicken meat and squeaked incessantly. The boy's shrieking had dwindled to a gaspy whimper, and he kept saying—or attempting to say—"please" and "God" and "Mama" over and over.

At last Jan was weary of it. He closed the lids on the two smaller boxes, and unlatched the big box and stood back, grasping his long stick heartily. Root Hughes clambered out quickly; he was bent nearly double, and his footing was extremely unsteady. He fell forward on his face into the litter of the stall floor; rose painfully. His face was white, electric with fear; his eyes were glassy like a bird's. The whole front of his clothing was wet—he had pissed himself thoroughly. He could not talk. He grabbed desperately in his mind for sense.

"I can still let them spiders out," Jan said. "They're just in them boxes there." He pointed with the stick.

For answer the boy vomited, soiling his galoshes, the bottoms of his trousers.

Jan watched dispassionately, thinking. Now his task was to get Root Hughes unseen on the road to his home and, after all, it didn't seem too difficult a problem. He brandished the stick. "I bet your mama's really going to lay into you when you get home," he said. "It's already way past suppertime."

TEN

THERE WAS A steady file of housekeepers. They came and went, usually they went away pretty quickly, within a week or so. Some of them the mother herself found unsatisfactory, but she never had to trouble to fire them. Uncle Hake made it unpleasant enough that they were eager to take themselves off, even if they happened to have pressing needs for a salary. He ran through housekeepers as some men would run through money. And every day he got more demanding, crabbier, and his perpetual belligerence began to have more edge, a bit more force to it. But maybe he had learned where to apply it more effectively. After all, a stupid man is often compensated for lack of intelligence by a generous share of animal cunning, especially if he has merely a mean soul.

One day in an August the war ended and everyone was joyful, went about shouting, shooting off guns and fireworks, banging on pans—anything to make a noise; they embraced one another and wept for happiness. But at the Anderson household it was as sullenly quiet as ever. (If it were not for Jan, it would have long ceased to be the Anderson household and would have become the Nolan household, with the mother's reserve of strength continually waning, seeping away as wastage, and with Uncle Hake gaining a firmer furtive toehold here and there. But Jan kept it honest Anderson; the uncle had stopped any direct attack on Jan, or on Timmie if there were a chance that the boy would hear about it. He kept his place. It was those eyes, those eyes.) V-J Day found Uncle Hake kicking about glumly in the lawn. His concern was that shiploads of returning heroes were going to wrest his job out of his rather limp grasp. He hated the job, true enough; but what kind of treatment was that? For a man who had slaved away his best years, working like a dog under a son of a bitch of a foreman, simply to be thrown away like a worn-out sock? The one speck of hope was that the job was so rotten nobody would want it, returning home. Not much hope. He poked disconsolately into the house, traipsing to the bathroom for a good stiff shot; hoped vaguely that he would run across the housekeeper so he could give her a piece of his mind.

Too late. This one had packed off for good an hour earlier.

The mother considered the prospects wearily. With husbands returning from the war, it was going to get continually more difficult to find help. And of course word about Uncle Hake had long ago got around and was still going around, venomous as ever. She drooped her high shoulders. The fiber was certainly weakening in her; sometimes her backbone seemed as frail as rotten string, and she felt she had gone all hollow inside. There was a shadow over all her body, and in this shadow were deeper shadows, under her dark eyes and under the chin now less firm than ever. Around her mouth and eyes her face was webby with tired fine little lines. And she simply would not allow herself to throw her weighty sorrow on the strength of Jan. In the first place she had no way of gauging that strength, and surely she couldn't trust it perfectly. She was sternly convinced that if her son were spent to the last milligram of his power, he would not say so. He was just silent, too silent for her to guess, certainly too silent to trust. If you tore his arms off his body he wouldn't make a peep. The other consideration was that Jan was already charged with Timmie: not unwillingly, of course, for he had taken this engagement upon himself early and silently. (Again, his silence.) He had begun to look out for the girl before even the mother had seen the need, and then later, when she had found out, she could not have relieved him even if she were strong enough. Timmie was already in too violent a symbiosis with the boy's will. Timmie's fierce attachment to Jan was a necessary piece of the fabric of the life of this family, and if it were disturbed the whole tottery edifice would fall in ruin. She did not consider whether Timmie's attachment and dependence might also be mortally important to Jan: his whole demeanor prevented such a thought. He seemed as self-sufficient as a mountain. She sighed again; her brave shoulders drooped even more. Sometimes it appeared to her clearly that ruin was the single destiny of the lot of them, but these thoughts she took care to put away. When it was possible. About her own future there was a curious heartbreaking blankness. She stared flatly at her husband's face in the photograph. Whether there was peace or not, there didn't seem to be much need to celebrate a victory.

It had been a various string of housekeepers. Mrs. Carr had been nervous as a sparrow, always overly busy, always twittering about—it had even annoyed her, the mother. Selma had been a slow mournful girl with all the cheering aspect of a black shroud; had a lover lost somewhere in the Normandy invasion. The religious zealot was Miz Blitters, who went about the house singing hymns and obviously disapproving their mistaken ways; she was always wrenching sharp shocking monosyllables out of Jan with her insistent catechizing. Miss Firestone, on the other hand, was as silent as the family among which she toiled, and that was the trouble: you kept finding her directly behind you when you thought you were alone; white-faced and taciturn, one Saturday night she ran away to South Carolina with an alcoholic house painter. Both Jan and Timmie accommodated them all: Jan, keeping to himself as entirely as possible, but forever watching out for his sister with meticulous attention, continually assuring, reassuring her; and Timmie, fearing and bewildered, and apparently becoming more and more distrustful, so that Jan became habitually ever more watchful and perhaps himself too distrustful.

For instance, he had almost—because of the misunderstanding of an instant—attacked the mother once. Poor Timmie's adolescence had sprung upon her like a tiger. Luckily it was the mother and not Jan who had discovered it. But it was he who discovered the mother kneeling at Timmie's feet wiping away the oily blood that streamed slow and thick on her legs. The girl was weeping, of course, sobbing without control, baffled, frightened terribly by the insulting slap her own soft body had delivered her. The mother too was weeping a little as she tried to soothe the daughter. "There there, there now, sweetheart, that's all right." It was merely a runic croon to keep away hysteria. And then Jan entered and she knew without turning from her sad task that it was he; and yet was so unprepared for the combative crackle of his snarl that she dropped the reddening washcloth.

"What are you doing to her?"

She turned to find herself facing without defense those blue eyes as belligerent as naked knives. And it was unfortunate that her voice wavered. "Nothing, Jan honey."

Again: *"What are you doing to her?"* And this time he took an admonishing step forward.

She hesitated, got a firmer grasp on her voice. "It's all right, Jan. It's just something that has to happen with girls. Timmie's going to be all right." She picked up the washcloth, turned back to the soft streaked legs. "Perhaps you had better go away for a little while," she said.

He too hesitated for a moment and then, apparently satisfied, acquiesced, wheeled about suddenly and went off.

She ministered to Timmie, getting her clean and neat. She put the dazed girl to bed and prepared warm cocoa for her. The girl lay white and guardedly in the crisp sheets. She clutched to her the stuffed giraffe of the fantastic aspect—the original cloth of Jannie's neck had worn through, and the mother had replaced it with red-

and-white-checked oilcloth, material which had advantages of cleanliness and durability. She gave the girl a last caring look, determined to have a talk with Jan.

Three or four times she called from the back door, and at last the blond son appeared in the dark doorway of the barn. He gave her a sweeping wave with his bony arm and started toward the house. She reflected. What in the world was so interesting in that old barn that Jan was so continually out there? Surely he was not simply engrossed with his own companionship. She ought really to investigate; it might be something dangerous or unhealthy. He could be playing with fire or with electricity. . . . But that wasn't like Jan. She decided to leave it alone. The boy had little enough peace.

She returned and sat at the dining-room table. When he came in she asked him to sit, which he did with a sort of deliberately awkward grace. Not really knowing how to begin, she gave some moments' attention to the backs of her thinning hands and then, after a quick hopeless glance at her husband's immobile pictured face, she said, "I want you to know how much I really do appreciate all the care you've been taking of Timmie."

He glanced at her, and for a moment she couldn't go on. As if to aid her, he cleared his throat.

"I feel that maybe you've been called on to do a job that might be too hard for your years." She halted again, certain that she had pitched herself a little too grandly. "Anyway, I'm sure you know what our problem is with Timmie. I'm afraid she's a little . . . slow."

He nodded, his face distantly troubled. "But she's good," he said, "she's real good."

"Oh yes, yes of course. Timmie's a good girl, I know that. But there is this . . . little problem with her, and

I think it's awfully fine of you to take care of her like you do. I'm awfully proud of you." She lifted her shadowy chin as if to demonstrate how proud she was.

He looked at the blue tablecloth as if there was a secret gospel woven among the threads.

"I'm afraid too that I haven't been doing my share for her. I know I haven't, really, but it's just almost impossible, really, what with my job at the plant and . . ." She paused, but she knew that she was telling him nothing new. She finished the sentence: ". . . and with your Uncle Hake."

"Yes," Jan said.

"What I wanted to tell you was, someday of course you'll be wanting to lead your own life."

He raised his eyebrows and she saw that he was genuinely puzzled. She took up his hand that was lying steady on the table and nodded assertively. "Yes, you will," she said. "Someday you're going to want to get married. I know you don't think so now, but someday you'll want to get married and you'll want a family of your own. And I want you to know that when that time comes you don't need to worry that you haven't done your duty toward Timmie. Goodness knows, you've done as much as a brother can do, and more. And if it turned out that you felt that Timmie ought to go away somewhere, to a good place, that would be perfectly all—"

"Go away where?" His eyes were wide.

"Well . . ." It was more delicate with him than she had guessed.

"She ain't going to go nowhere," he said.

"Maybe so, but if it happened that—"

"There ain't nothing going to happen like that. She ain't going to go nowhere." His voice was rich but flat, unyielding as brass. He stood, scraping the wicker-bottomed chair back, but she still held his hand and she pulled him, refractory, to her, embraced his excited chest to her shoulder. "Oh Jan," she cried, "what's going to become of you?"

He squirmed out of her grasp, startled.

She too was surprised. She had thought she was going to say, "What's going to become of us?" But she had omitted herself. "Go on, go on and play," she said hoarsely. "I don't know what I'm thinking of."

"All right," he said, and left. But first he went through the hall and slipped Timmie's door open, checking.

She heard him close the back door as he went outside. Undoubtedly he was going back to the barn. She held her face in her hands. Things were all backwards. It was an ability of Jan's to comfort Timmie, and yet when the mother had intended to give the boy confidence she had ended by frightening him, or at least by startling him. Uncle Hake, who she had hoped when she had invited him in would stand in the house for a sort of phony father, was without authority, and in fact—she was thankful for it—he was thoroughly cowed by Jan. Her own place she couldn't define so easily: she just seemed to be the lady who kept the engine lubricated, rather obscure in her house in a decade when women had become very much in evidence. She pressed her dark hair back; these days it seemed to be thinning; in the mornings she found linear tangles of it in comb and brush. Tiredness never left her any more; it had settled on her like a biting dark frost. She felt she could tumble into sleep for ages. Sleeping Beauty? She smiled an unsatisfactory smile.

And yet she was still a pretty lady. Her increasing

paleness, even the darknesses in her face, suited her well, giving her an old-fashioned air, rather like the well-bred ladies of the mid-nineteenth century, those you might read about in *Villette*. Though drooping slightly, her carriage was still light and graceful and the faint stoop actually added a pleasing asymmetry to her body in those fashionable rigid suits with the soldierly shoulders. She was much too thin, but it showed only in her legs, which were also beginning to get a little veiny; only to the touch could she be discovered as gaunt. The dimnesses beneath her jaw line served actually to set off the smooth oval face. Her lips were regular, not too full, and her dark eyes were bright, but perhaps this was not healthy.

She glanced at the unchanging face of Robert and after a moment of strange resolution she rose and went to the picture and took it up. With the forearm of the sleeve of her suit she wiped a light film of dust from the glass. Then she took the photograph to a cabinet and put it into a drawer face down. After all, the war was over. She closed the drawer. Now she felt weirdly displaced. She removed the picture and set it back again but it was no use, the move had been made. She closed the cabinet drawer on it again.

She went into the kitchen and gathered the silver into a big glittery pile and began to polish it. Despite her weariness it seemed better to keep working. As she worked she thought about Timmie and Hake and mostly about Jan. For herself—there seemed nothing to think about.

ELEVEN

THEN WHEN he was fourteen his sister had become mad. Jan went through the rooms of the house gathering objects with sharp points, pens, pencils, paring knives, needles. Scissors he broke off half along the length. And all these things he hid in the barn or threw away. At first she had got everything sharp and tried to pierce the palms of her hands and her feet at a point just below the cuneiform bone. And then it was Jan she wanted to wound in those places. He had been more surprised than frightened or injured when his body was jolted by the open safety pin she had pushed half through the palm of his left hand. All the while, she searched his face, her dark eyes burning and xanthic in the orange light of the sunset coming through the west window. He withdrew the pin and regarded her sadly. She smiled: it was like that; whenever Jan was sad she smiled, and when his face was happy hers became mournful. He planned to keep every emotion away from his features.

Another queer thing: she had always been slow, but now with her madness her intelligence had grown greater. She could plan things now and she noticed if she was being watched. He had to sneak to check on her and sometimes, if he were employed upon something that would keep him busy alone for a while, he would lock her in her room; and this began to require ingenuity. She did not like to be locked up and she seemed to be able to sense when it was going to happen, and then there was no coaxing her into her room. Her room; it was all hers now: Jan slept in the living room on the dim sofa which let down the back. The sofa he didn't mind, nor sleeping in the living room, where he was awakened early every morning by Uncle Hake—there was nothing gentle about the way he was awakened. But he regretted not being able to be with Timmie during the night. Yet it was clearly impossible. Each night she was locked in the little bedroom amid a terrific fuss and she would screech and bang against the door. It was a terrifying sound. Jan lay awake far into the night watching through the wide living-room windows the stars glinting fitfully or the bleached C of the moon. Even now he watched the universe without rancor; he loved his sister more fiercely and more steadily than ever.

He tried to plan, but nothing sensible would come clear in his head. He even thought once of questioning the mother, but out of habit he rejected the impulse. It

83

was evident that he had to do something, and he became continually more angry with the brain that was no help to him. The mother had had to absolve herself of the problem: any step she might take would probably give hurt to Jan—he had made this clear. But still, but still . . . He resolved to take a firmer grip on even the least of his actions and thoughts and to watch out more carefully for Timmie. Obviously, it was now a matter of grasping the first happy opportunity that might break. In the meantime he had to keep things tight, severe.

But nothing fortunate broke. The various transient housekeepers were quite afraid of the girl, and Jan suspected that when he was away in school they were cruel to her. When he had the chance he examined the girl's arms and legs for marks. Uncle Hake too he had to watch. The dingy little man did not talk against the girl any more, but on his face there was an expression of grim good humor, as if he had achieved a secret victory. Jan knotted his fists, ground them against his belly. All his worst premonitions were coming true.

He asked if she wanted to hear about Peter Rabbit.

"No," she said. "He doesn't have covers on his eyes."

"You mean when Peter's in bed asleep."

"No. Covers over his *eyes*." She put a finger on the head of Mr. McGregor. The irascible old gentleman was wearing spectacles.

"Those are his glasses," he said.

Familiar authority was in her face. "You better have covers over your eyes," she said.

"How come I ought to wear glasses?"

"So they wouldn't hurt my head." With both soiled hands she touched her cheeks gently. "Your eyes hurt my head because you don't have covers."

He managed to procure from a dime store a pair of glasses, steel-framed, the lenses pure window glass. He wore them whenever he was about Timmie, and for some reason they seemed to make her gay. "All the big pink birds wear glasses now," she told him. And in a way the glasses did lessen the unnerving impact of his gaze, and when he had to deal with Uncle Hake he found that he removed them. It was a curious circumstance: it was the first time he was aware of his eyes. From the toy giraffe the glass eyes had long ago been lost, but she made him draw with a pencil circles where the eyes had been and lines going back to where ears never were. Now Jannie too wore glasses.

"Are you all right?" he asked her.

"No. I feel bad."

"What's the matter?"

"I feel real bad. Because my arm hurts where she bit me."

This would be Miss Firestone, the new silent one.

"Let me see," he said. "Where did she bite you?" He took her arm, but she jerked it violently away. "Here, let me see. I ain't going to bite you."

At last she let him look.

"I don't see where," he said. He let her arm drop. "I don't see no place she bit you."

"Because she bit it off, she bit it all off." Her voice was angry and she was slyly happy.

This was not madness, but perversity. He was intensely troubled. Why was it that he didn't understand any more? The tighter his will got, the more easily she was able to evade its grasp. The closer his surveillance of her became, the more he felt, though obscurely, that she was watching back.

TWELVE

IN THE WIND the fluffy pink birds with Jan's eyes and penciled-on spectacles, in the sky the flags of thin bleeding flesh . . . Her vision was expectant, insistent. She knew how the world cheated parsimoniously, squandering all upon her soft poor body. . . . New vertigoes were demanded, demanding. It was the arctic solitudinous kiss of being watched. Abrasion of kindly eyes across the grain of her dependence. Didn't the gray shadows of the room escalate into sun-drenched terraces? The purpose of her affections: to escape love . . . She possessed no presentiment of freedom.

———

The door had its mouth clipped shut; but then would come the dry chuckle of the seeking key and the door mouth would boom wide with laughter, showing Jan, its blond tongue like a pale flame. Because she had made him blind, hiding away his eyes, she would not talk to her brother, but only giggle. It was planned. She giggled, looking at her hand, a nest of white eyeless worms chained to the future red rose. She felt that she alone had invented the terrifying price of devotion.

She had got smarter. Time did not drip away any longer; had frozen it solid, like a block of glass around the house. She had trapped the others in unmoving. Jan stood transfixed in the mouth of the door; he too opened his mouth. Because he used to bite mice his words changed into gray mice and fell and ran cheeping around the room, round and round. These beasts were frightened of her. On Jan's palms and on his feet burned the roses which he did not see. She had made him blind, hoarded away his fighting eyes. In the great block of ice everything was trapped, even the firm clean bones of the mother. She had made it clear that all vistas of movement, all the comedies of mutation, were to be seen from outside; she would protect them, keep Jan viciously close to her love. They were objects like stuffed toys. Only she herself would be allowed the worshiping of Jannie.

In the wind the heavy phantoms of desire: especially the mother, whose sweet body drifted slightly with unwilled change; filmy she was, cool as the underbelly of a pillow. Along her high bright esplanade the girl wandered, perceiving the family sprawled out below her like an earthwork of vermin laid open. She alone knew the joyous rage of her sun. With her hand outstretched she could keep them in an ignorant shadow, and if she drew her hand to herself the light would fall blinding and parching upon them, so that they must kneel, praying to her once again to restore to them their brutish obscurity. It was clearly simple, it was totally planned. She had gathered to her her own thoughts, those floating fluffy pink birds camouflaged with the emblem of blindness. Or she could descend the solid gray shadows of the little room to walk divinely with them. She would give them speech, piercing rosy mouths into their hands and feet. They couldn't imagine the warm simple things that love would tell them: it was because their hands too were blind, and they had covered away the seeing of their feet. She was entirely enlightened; from her mouth emanated tuneful perfumes.

In the air was a yellow sweat that soaked into the body. She could clap the ear of her hand to her vagina and hear the shrieking of the blood.

She had locked the house in a Sunday afternoon of ten years ago.

Everything that was going to happen was filled with anticipation.

She pirouetted, holding her skirt aloft. A mournful waltz. She felt airy and happy and she raised her face to take in the breeze her dancing had started up. It was like a sweet pure hand on her face; it did not wish to protect but only to caress her. With the pure living air she could feel safe. She too was the air, soft and uncaring, yet germane, causative. Everything would happen as she conceived. It was clear that the mother would die; she would be only clean glassy bones and the ghost of her in the wind would go blind and faceless. This was what came of being without desire; desirelessness was blindness, wasn't it? Everything was shamelessly true. The elusion of the love that suffocated to kill: this was the purpose of true premonitions—to escape future happening because of its boring certainty. The mother would die away, already she was empty as a lampshade. Her soul, a charged muskiness, would haunt the air for a while; the mother had practiced for a long time the art of almost bodiless persistence. But at last every vestige would disappear; she would make the wind purer by entering into it. Her skirt touched her soft pink knees and she ceased to dance. She hid her face in her deafened hands. With her eyes she followed the ascent of the gray shadows through the vague ceiling to where the sun rolled red in the sky, a flamy wound. Absolute zones of clearness threatened her supremacy, but then she really pretended to nothing more than understanding. Actually, it was the sky that was fatuous. The corners of her mind peeped their eyes; it was happening now: the door mouth gave its metallic snicker and then opened to disclose its blond tongue. "Are you all right?" Jan said. She giggled, giggled, looked at her white hands, a cluster of struggling blind worms. He went away, the door swallowed him back, snickering again, again tickled by the clumsy key. In a while he would pop through once more like a coo-coo in a clock. She closed her eyes and began to steady the room back from where Jan's weighty presence in the threshold had tilted it over. The breeze had stopped, the pink floating birds were tumbling. She grasped her mind dispassionately, causing the birds to dip up, to fly whirling about like drunken kites. Because she had slipped away Jan's bad eyes she would give him eyes at hand and foot. He would perceive gratefully; she knew her power over him; she knew that he had found her watching his own watching, and as a sentinel he was no longer alone, not so entirely lonely now. But this frightened him—he was now lonesome for his former loneliness. He had lived too long under the paw of that one big tiger, his will.

Soundless gray roads streaked the sky. A yellow stone idol crouched in the field of sagegrass: it was the brother that Jan had created from the stone he used to worship. She could see that this stone image would one day overtake Jan and crush him mortally to itself. Because she had blinded him he could now not see how the clean path he had laid was curling back upon itself under his feet. Still, it was better this way; with his life gone he would be loose from the tyranny he had created, that tyranny which she was beginning to subsume. She comprehended that she could not topple the machine of his will; it had been too furiously formed too long ago.

Jan's real home was in the east, swarmed over by flocks of yellow beech leaves flying in the October wind. It was a long way. The gray silent road led through dull miles of swamp and diseased water. Abandoned barns guarded the hilltops, and among the rafters of them sat rows of owls. In the brackish light their eyes were mean, feral. They spoke but one killing word; *croo,* they said to one another, winking black eyelids. Even from the outermost ramparts of her bright celestial ledges Timmie could not see this place; she knew of it only because the part of her that Jan carried unwittingly about with him could perceive. Such a dismal track the whole journey was: there was nothing green, nothing shiny at all. The skies were dirt-colored, the sun was always exiled. At an ever-decreasing distance, the mountains were barren, hooting with cold wind. And then the house, the windows blinded, shutters hanging awry, the cold wind blowing the trees gauntly naked, the grounds strewn with sharp stones. And yet in the attic window a white sweet darkened face whisked across, the musky ghost of the mother. On the porch an empty rocking chair was tipped back and forth by the wind, rocking emptily without stop. Belligerently recalcitrant, the lock hardly admitted the key and, upon entering, her brother always found room after empty room patched with ripped wallpaper, and the tar-colored maws of disused fireplaces. Hollow-sounding hallways, corners slithery with brass-headed snakes. Eyed bits of uncovered window which brought the bony landscape closer. Flights of stairs rottenly uncertain. As he climbed higher it got darker. The key to the attic door would not fit. When he turned to come down again the stories below were as deep and dark and fatal as a dry well. On the stairway he found the S-shaped bone of an unknown venomous animal. —And yet her brother was not frightened, but resigned. He, darkling, gravely expected what she so clearly foresaw. She did not find it queer that she only understood the future that Jan tried to deny: she understood only true things. Her brother's brave dreams escaped her, they were misty and luminous and wishful—the products of the created will, not of the unwillingly sentient desire. . . . She lay down on the bed and began to make love to Jannie, saying queer tender words.

THIRTEEN

Uncle hake gave Lora Bowen a pinch—not too hard; he knew the limits.

"Oh," she said. "You better cut that out." She turned to face him, holding up the hot iron, and she made a slight move as if to touch him with it. She was smiling; she had one of those saturninely humorous faces in which the corners of the mouth turned down with a smile.

Uncle Hake sniggered and caressed the knuckles of one hand with the greasy palm of the other. He shuffled away, his slippers making an oily rasp on the worn linoleum. In a while he would return for another pinch.

Lora Bowen was the last in a long unsuccessful line of housemaids, the only one, for Uncle Hake's money, who wasn't too worthless to shoot. Actually she was a wild tough girl from far back in some distant hollow of the hills, but she was tartly pretty and mischievous. "Full of life," Uncle Hake said. She didn't seem to mind him either, and it was possible that somewhere on the rancid old man she had got a whiff of money. She had crisp red hair, a double handful of freckles, eyes green as bits of green glass. She was short and rather broad-shouldered, held herself erect; had a middling slender waist. Like a pretty thoroughbred mare she had slim ankles and was muscular in the hams. She kept herself alert too, didn't miss a trick; hadn't been in the house a week before she saw just how things were lined up, but she held her own counsel and kept her eyes open. It wasn't too hard for the family to see what was going on behind that sharp pert face. She was nineteen years old.

Jan was on shaky ground anyway, and this new girl left him at a slight loss. She worked hard, with fair success, at treating the strange blond boy with cool laughing condescension. She couldn't quite stand firm against those blunt eyes, but she managed most of the time to get by him without encountering them. That was her real talent: she could slip by; with some effort and a spoonful of shortening she could probably ease through a keyhole. She too knew the limits: as much as possible she kept away from Timmie, and when it was not possible to give the girl berth she treated her with painstaking reverence. This manner was to mollify the brother and in some measure to take him off guard, for although she didn't often encounter those blue eyes there was no mistaking the force of them. For herself, Lora didn't mind the mad girl one way or another. She didn't fear her; poor Timmie didn't even give her the creeps. Thrown suddenly into that weird household, Lora probably found that Timmie differed from the others only in degree.

Lora was a good enough worker, and she had a cunning good nature—which made up for a great deal. She lacked Mrs. Boggs's thorough lumbering efficiency, but she got the house clean at least once every three days and got it in order at least once each day. Somehow she had persuaded Uncle Hake not to make too extensive a litter by the easy chair in the living room. She was quick too, and came up with much free time. Part of this time she spent in private researches of her own which the mother and the uncle guessed at, but which they felt powerless and, really, unconcerned to stop. If she wanted to pry into their affairs that was *her* affair. They had no designs or business other than those which were plainly seen by anyone who cared to. The family was secretive by nature, not because it had secrets. At any rate, the sharp-faced girl was soon satisfied and after her work she would sit on the sofa in the living room to read the newspaper, or get into verbal (and sometimes physical) horseplay with Uncle Hake.

"Law, what are you saying?" She pushed his whispering round face away from her ear and regarded him with her shiny green eyes. "You ought to be ashamed, an old feller like you."

"I ain't so old as you think, honey," said Uncle Hake. "You come over here and I'll show you how old I am."

"Well, I don't know what to say to *that*."

"Come on over here a minute," he said gaily.

"I ain't coming over there a bit. I don't trust you, that's why."

"Well, that proves I ain't so old then, don't it?"

She uttered a deep flattering laugh. Her green eyes glittered like glass beads. "Well, I ain't coming over there to find out."

"I bet you don't have to find out much," he said. On his face was an obviously calculating expression. "I bet there's not much you don't know."

She lifted her chin sharply, giving the crisp red hair a toss. "I guess that's none of your beeswax, corn bread, or shoe tacks," she said.

"I bet it's true, though."

"What'll you bet?"

"I bet a pretty. I'll bet a hundred dollars."

"Well, give it to me then. You lose."

"How am I supposed to know whether? Have to try it out first, to see if you're telling the truth."

"You better stay over there and stick to your knitting, I believe."

He made a tentative lunge at her and with the toe of her black loafer she gave him a gentle playful kick in the balls. He stopped where he was and opened his eyes wide. "Well, that proves it," he said. "That proves you know more than you let on like."

She folded her arms, crossed her legs, and stared him down with the bright eyes. "I guess I don't know what in the world you're talking about," she said.

He rose and shuffled across to the soiled easy chair and slumped into it. He took a cigar from his pocket and zipped off the cellophane. "You're a teaser," he said. "I never seen such a teaser in my life." He lit the cigar.

She regarded him for a moment, tapping her lively foot. "Well, you can sit around all day and smoke them old cigars, but I got work to do." She went out, found a dustcloth, returned and began industriously to polish at the undernourished bookcase across the room. In comradely insult she jiggled her fanny at him.

He watched, puffing the fumy cigar. This was the kind of housecleaning Uncle Hake appreciated.

The mother observed this sort of scene—there was no attempt to hide it from her—with some trepidation. It seemed to her to represent the rooting-in of one more force over which she had no control. Uncle Hake was lonely, of course, lonelier even than Jan, since Jan really expected nothing else. He had few amusements outside the house except for the occasional weekend poker games, and his only diversions within were his bottle in the medicine chest and his own petulance. Lora Bowen had got past his orneriness easily enough, and to the mother it seemed that her brother's loneliness was pretty large capital for the red-haired girl to build upon. She permitted herself a slight smile, and shrugged. She didn't even feel justified in mentioning her thoughts to her brother.

"Ow. You cut that out." It was Lora in the living room. "I sure would hate to've been your sister," she said. "I never seen such a man to go slapping and pinching."

"That wasn't no kind of a slap you'd give your sister." Uncle Hake admitted it gaily.

"Well, I guess not," she said. "If it was, she wouldn't have lived to get knee high. One of these first days I'll give you a dose of your own medicine and we'll see how you like that."

"Well, I've got some real medicine for you too. You ought to try some one time."

"What kind of medicine you talking about?"

"Good for what ails you."

"Well, I ain't ailing," she said. "I'm a healthy girl."

He looked her over from red hair to black loafers. "Yeah," he said, "I guess you're right."

Jan too observed these scenes, rather dourly. Something disturbing was rising within him, gathering itself about the core of his fifteen years. He was losing ground, and now he found in himself an unsuspected agency which he had never been required to attempt to control. By way of experiment he found Lora mopping the kitchen and he gave her a pat on her cheerful buttocks. The result wasn't particularly gratifying.

She waited until she had got her face furious, and then turned toward him. "You better keep your damn hands to yourself, young man, and I mean it," she said. "You just better not give me any trouble, or you'll really have trouble." She talked on like that for a while, calling him "young man" and "Buster-boy," threatening to tell his mother.

This latter warning didn't weigh too heavily with him, but he was bothered by the unsuccess of the trial and by the fact that he had betrayed himself into making it. It was indubitably a genuine betrayal, in fact a mistake of the sort that he never permitted. He saw it as a symptom of a wider disease of his condition, and he felt strongly a need to correct this state. But he was completely darkling about which way to turn, any manner in which to set to work. He retreated in painful confusion, not looking at her, not looking to either side. He went out the back door, going to the barn to think.

Lora stroked her freckled neck, greatly relieved. She had figured her risk and had taken it; she had been absolutely uncertain how the son would react. For all she

knew, he might have jumped her like an animal. . . .
No, she could see that that wasn't his way, and even
after her tirade, she knew she was still going to keep clear
of him. Yet, as she watched him retreating, a new recog-
nition realized itself in her green luminous eyes, and she
gave a faint nod. Her mind was laboring away, as pre-
cisely as a sewing machine punching stitches into cloth.
More than she had thought Jan was something to reckon
with, but now she fancied she had found a handle.

Uncle Hake continued to have clear—but careful—
sailing with her. "Come in my room a minute," he said.
"I got something to give you."

"I got something to give your room too," she said, "and
that's a good cleaning. 'Course you ain't going to let me
do that."

"Ain't no need for you to clean it."

"Well, you just don't know how good and straight I
can make up a bed."

"I'm more interested in the way you can tear one up,"
he said. The old man was becoming a positive wit. It was
worth the effort; her flattering rich laugh delivered him
into a paroxysm of glee. He patted her near thigh.

"I declare you ought to been a baker, the way you're
always pinching and pounding me like I was a big gob
of dough."

They even began to fall into serious talk. She had
asked him about the job he detested (of course, he had
not lost it, after all his fretting), and he naturally didn't
want to look small in her eyes. He explained it in great
detail, and at the last added a eulogium to the importance of the task. "If it wasn't for me and the others in
there," he said, "that mill would lose all kinds of money.
Because if that stuff wasn't tested out right and they run

off a big batch of it, they'd have to get rid of every last bit of it, just throw it away. It'd cost thousands and thousands of dollars."

"That really sounds complicated," she said. "I guess you have to be real smart to work in there."

"Nah." He could deny her statement, but he added, "You have to be on your toes, though."

"It sounds like a lot of responsibility."

"I reckon," he said. And then the notion struck him that it really was a responsibility.

"Well, it's more'n I'd want. I want to be foot-loose and fancy free, myself."

He was beginning to acquire such a new edge to his sensibilities that he suspected in this remark an ironic suggestion, but he couldn't puzzle it out. "How come?" he said.

She stretched carelessly, holding her arms above her head. Her yellow sweater crept up, disclosing an inch or two of bare midriff. "That's the way I am," she said. "I want to be as free as the wind. I want to be ready to go any time."

"Well, I'm ready to go. Any time you want."

She gave him a limp backhand gesture. "You ain't never got but one thing on your mind."

"Well, what's wrong with that? I bet you can't think of nothing better."

"You be surprised the things I think of."

"Like what?"

"Oh, I ain't going to tell you that," she said. "It'd spoil it all to tell it too soon."

Perhaps unknowingly, Lora lavished most of her housekeeping upon the mother's bedroom. Understandably: it was the one room in the house which could possibly some day be made cheerful. It faced the east, the bright morning, and the window in the right wall let in the early-afternoon sunshine. The dressing table was skirted with a pretty bright chintz. The wallpaper was light blue with a silver-colored delicate floral tracery. Three light-blue throw rugs were disposed at the dressing table and at the right side and at the foot of the bed. The bed itself, always cleanly formal with a white chenille spread, had four tall maple posts; Lora felt that with some ingenuity she could stretch a canopy there—a pleasant thought which reminded her somehow of the photographs of sailboats. At core her nature longed for light cleanliness, and this was the single room that released her vague desires. Not that it was at all blithe now; it was too bare, really naked in fact; it needed more . . . well, more junk. Bric-a-brac. Something to show that it was inhabited by a nice lady, and not by a prisoner or a saint. Lora paused in washing the east windows to gaze at the top of the maple chest of drawers; she nodded, she knew exactly what needed to go there to give the room more character, or, rather, a different character: Lora's own, and not the mother's.

Timmie's room she cleaned as best she could, taking great pains not to disturb the girl more than was needful, and contriving always to work facing the girl, never turning her back upon her. She was not afraid of Timmie, but she was cautious; it was almost as if she was cleaning the cage for a partially domesticated bear. When Jan wasn't in school when she cleaned Timmie's room, he was present, silent and watchful, but not unobtrusive —that boy could never be unobtrusive. She fell into the habit of working there only when she knew Jan could be present. The girl was different then. She actually exhibited a different physical aspect when Jan was absent: you noticed how large her body was, and how strong underneath the softness. But in Jan's presence both Timmie's size and strength seemed diminished. Lora did not reflect too heavily upon these matters; she was pragmatic. Whatever it was between brother and sister, it had been going on too long for her to tamper with or even to understand. But she could perceive that there was more gesture of dominion than actual mastery on the part of Jan; obviously the alliance between them had changed somehow; it seemed—perhaps—that what had once been necessity had now become a difficult game. At any rate, Timmie seemed now toying with her brother in a sort of open furtiveness. Lora let it drop. No point in perplexing herself to no end. She chuckled as she pushed the dust mop along the baseboard: what a queer crazy family she had let herself into.

Well, Uncle Hake was easy enough to understand. She slapped his hovering hand away from her left breast. "I declare I'm going to the sheriff's and get me a pair of handcuffs," she said. "I'm going to chain you to the bedpost."

"Huh," he said, "bedpost would be all right, if you going to keep me company."

"You don't need no company," she said. "Do you good to let you alone to think about your sins."

"Huh, sins. I bet if you thought about your sins it'd take a good long while to get 'em thought. About ten years, I guess."

"Speak for yourself, John Alden," she said. "You don't even know what you're talking about."

"Huh, say I don't," he said.

"That's right," she said.

"I guess I seen girls before like you are. I guess you ain't all the Miss Priss you make out like you are."

"Law, just listen to the old man talk, just goes on and on."

"I'm right, though. You're one of them girls that talks like you was born in Sunday school, but when you get them out in the right place at the right time they're just like wildcats. Tear a man to pieces."

"Maybe you know somebody like that." She thickened her voice with high scorn. "That's just the kind of a girl I guess you *would* know."

"All alike, you're all alike," he said. "Act like you've got a ramrod up your—"

"You better hush right there," she said.

". . . but you'd come down off of your high horse pretty quick." He waggled his soiled head. "Don't think I can't see through you easy enough."

"I sure am glad I don't see the things you think you see. I declare you've got the evilest mind of any one man I ever seen."

"No I ain't. I just got the natural notions of a man. And I can tell you them's the same notions as women's got too."

"Huh."

"Huh yourself. You know I'm saying the truth, as sure as you're standing there."

"You think so, huh?"

"Well, ain't it the truth?" He waited, expecting confirmation of his fine dialectic victory.

She made out as if reflecting. "Maybe so," she said. "But before that, I'd have to be wearing something right here." With the thumb and forefinger of her right hand she pulled her ring finger vertical like a stiff sentry. He

102

looked at it dumbly, and she turned away from him, going toward the kitchen.

He spoke to her rigorous retreating back. "Before that what?"

She turned, leveling her bright green stare on his face. "What do you think?" she said. "I mean, before I'd let any damn man have a piece." She left the room.

He sniggered in complete surprise, his mouth partially open. With the greasy nail of a forefinger he scratched the base of his skull where the glimmering of an idea had signaled an itch.

FOURTEEN

Jan's hair had darkened. It glinted, the color of late sagegrass, in the mild sunlight that streamed through the chinks between the boards of the barn. The horse trough that he had once converted into a man-trap now served him as a storage chest. He kept all kinds of things: lengths of string and wire, a number of paring knives, usable flashlight batteries, nails of various kinds and sizes, a hammer with a refitted handle, three pistol bullets lying in a bath of oil—anything that might conceivably be useful at any time. And he kept nothing that was not useful. It was almost as if he were building an ark before a deluge—he was so concerned with equipment, so much at the mercy of premonitions. He breathed deeply through his nose, tasting with the roof of his mouth the warmth of the air and the musty stillness of the somnolent barn. He grasped the top board of the stall wall where it had been worn slick long ago by hands bigger and tougher at palm than his own. The solidity of the wood was almost gratifying; it indicated that the world of things, of everything, wasn't so tenuous and ambiguous as he was now continually perceiving it. The wood had a will, firm, friendly opposed—the gratification came from the fact that very little of what he had now to try to master responded to the manipulations of his own will. It was all bodiless situation. With objects he was on firm ground. He lowered himself to the littered earth floor and drew one knee up to rest his chin, letting the other crooked knee lie flat in the dust and old straw. He looked like an anomalous Orpheus, the leather thongs of his high-topped shoes serving for mute harp strings. Not entirely mute: his mind went round and round in a despairing fugue, no beginning and no ending. Mostly his difficulty was (he thought) that problems no longer had definite edges: blowsy intimations which seemed as if they could in an instant distill to catastrophe. He sighed murmurously. Everything was evading the grasp of his mind and coming under the control of his body, that wearying machine he comprehended only dimly. He had begun to desire, he had come to the age for it, and this was totally the error of his body—which he wished he could shuck away, seeing that he was so much stronger naked of it. Another problem was his lack of perception—that faculty which had formerly been so discerning was now choked. He reasoned at it and produced two possible causes: Timmie, through whom he had used to understand so much, had largely closed herself to him, and, worse, she was peering out at him. She understood not Jan, but Jan's manner of knowledge better than he did, and in some way she was taking advantage of this and he could not even discover to what purpose. And his will, that mechanism he had fashioned so intently and so finely to see with seemed now to be blocking the clear sight of another better perceptive faculty within him that he knew nothing of. He was blocking his own view. . . . He rubbed his stiff yellow eyebrows with the heel of his palm and absently ran a finger against the grain of the fine yellow whiskers that were beginning to appear on his cheeks. He was at a complete loss. He could formulate all the tasks which he thought loomed for him to overcome, but he knew that this would be to violate them: he would in fact be willing them into shape, squeezing them out of the amorphous into the definite—while this amorphousness was actually the real nature of the problems, or at least a great part of them. Round and round . . . He hugged his left knee to his chest, speculating on what he might now be able to do if so long ago he had not formed himself so fiercely, so steadily, into what he was. But if he hadn't done so, would Timmie, or the both of them for that matter, would they have survived? He shrugged, despairing. It was like what Uncle Hake was always saying: "If I'd of knew then what I know now. . . ." Again he stroked his finger against the grain of his incipient beard. He determined to put anything into its stupidest, most brutal form; and the thought came to him like a dark boat nosing out of a fog bank. Much of the trouble was in the fact that he wanted to fuck Lora Bowen.

FIFTEEN

ONE FRIDAY EVENING about a month later Uncle Hake went off—presumably to play poker—and he didn't return until Monday morning, shortly before the hour he had to report to work. He brought Lora with him; it had been her weekend off. They came in together, standing in the living-room doorway as stiff and sharply awkward as if they were figures on a daguerreotype, and together confronted Jan and the mother. Now they were man and wife. They were both dressed in good Sunday clothes—Uncle Hake even looked washed—and on the red-haired girl's ring finger there glittered a band and cool white stones. At last Uncle Hake's miserliness had come to some purpose. He observed closely the polished toes of his black shoes and showed in his red face a pain-ful grin. He spoke to the mother. "Well, Jenny," he said, "I hope you're going to wish us luck."

She paused; she had to suppress the impulse to rush to her brother, embracing him and comforting him with the same words she had formerly offered Timmie: "There now, darling, it'll be all right." But she stood firm and spoke in a tight many-colored voice. "Of course. You know I do, Hezekiah Nolan."

There was a long unnerving silence.

Then Lora spoke, her voice soft, actually meek. "I guess I ought to told you, Miz Anderson. I'm sorry about that, that I didn't tell you I wouldn't be here to work no more."

"Of course not, honey. You're one of the family now." The mother made one uncertain step forward, and then the two women came together as suddenly as a handclap. "Oh honey, oh honey," said the mother. Over all her face were the small tears. They hugged each other tightly, like persons overturned from a raft in the middle of the ocean; they patted each other's shoulders softly and rhythmically. "Oh honey," the mother said.

"I just hope we didn't hurt your feelings," Lora said. "I told Hake we ought to tell you first beforehand."

"That's all right. Oh honey . . . That's perfectly all right."

Jan and Uncle Hake stood apart shamefaced, as if, tieless, they had just been denied admittance to a formal restaurant.

At last the women separated and stood gazing mo-mentarily at each other in a sorrowing fondness. Then the mother smiled, and Lora grinned, showing the whole front of her strong white teeth.

"Yes, it's a surprise," said the mother. "It's a complete surprise, but it's a happy one."

Uncle Hake cleared his throat gruffly. "Actually, Jenny, we—I'd of told you except I wasn't real sure how you'd take it."

"I couldn't think of a better way to tell me than just to surprise me," she said in a high clear voice—in which Jan recognized an undertone of sharp sorrow which had just now entered into it. "And Jan too." She turned to him. "Aren't you happy for them, sweetheart?" She gestured toward Lora, who was now composed, perhaps even relaxed. "This is your Aunt Lora now, you know."

"Yes," Jan said.

Lora smiled at him and Jan took off his unmagnifying square glasses and looked straight through her candescent eyes. She flushed to an embarrassed color and quickly averted her gaze, staring at Jan's darkened blond hair. She felt that Jan had read too much with the one sharp strike through her eyes; but in the next moment the advantage was hers.

The mother asked brightly, "Aren't you going to kiss your new aunt, Jan?"

The question so bewildered him that he even took a slight backward step. "No," he said. He rubbed the lenses of his glasses on a shirt sleeve.

And Lora advanced, her arms spread out. "Not kiss me, Jan? You're going to hurt my feelings doing like that."

He was entirely frightened. If he had known how, he would have essayed a joke. "No, I can't do that."

"Why, Jan, sweetheart," said the mother.

"I guess I'm just not his type," Lora said. "I'm just not pretty enough to suit Jan."

Uncle Hake's voice was phlegmy. "Honeybabe," he said, "you're pretty enough for anybody in this world, pretty as a picture."

"Not for him, anyhow," she said, pointing a steady finger at Jan's confused head.

Still facing them, he retreated. Then he turned, and at the back door he broke into a gangly run, scuttered out of the house away over the lawn. The laughter of the three rose behind him like a wash of tide.

But in a while he returned, steady with himself, and careful. He seemed to have become reconciled to things. They had made breakfast, and now over the soiled plates and the half-filled coffee cups Uncle Hake was telling all the adventures of the bus trip to Spartanburg, South Carolina.

"But it was so inconvenient," the mother said. "If I'd only known, you could have taken the car. Those bus rides are always so terrible." The quavery note of sorrow had congealed already in her voice to become an element of its timbre—Jan noted it, fearful of all portents.

Uncle Hake tipped back in the chair, talking around the foul drooping cigar. "Oh, it wasn't so bad, was it?" He winked at his bride, a wink as heavy as a dictionary.

"It wasn't bad at all, the trip I mean. Of course, those bus stations are just such awful places all the time," Lora said. She told the story. In the Spartanburg depot a drunk soldier had made a pass at her and Uncle Hake had had to get the ticket seller to make the fellow leave her alone.

Without moving his head Jan nodded to himself, watching Uncle Hake closely through the silly glasses. The old man seemed unconcerned by what was clearly —to Jan, at any rate (he tried, but couldn't catch Lora's eye; she was intently avoiding his gaze)—a recital of his own cowardice. He wagged his head, sagely confirming the several points in his wife's story.

She brought it to a gay end. "But that's the only bad thing that happened the whole time."

Uncle Hake spoke as if he were imitating Democritus. "Can't take a long trip like that without expecting something to happen," he said. He leaned forward in the chair and the whitish burden of cigar ash spilled on his vested paunch. "One more cup of coffee and I got to get to work. I didn't ask for no time off for a honeymoon, but I figure I will a little later on."

The mother half rose, but Lora laid a restraining hand on her shoulder. "You just set still," she said, "and I'll get it. I guess I better get used to waiting on my old man."

While Lora was in the kitchen the mother leaned toward her brother and said in a soft low murmur, "You're fifty-two years old, Hake, you're fifty-two."

He brushed an angry hand through a drift of cigar smoke. "I guess I know that, I guess I know what I'm doing."

"All right," she said, and she never again spoke to him about the matter. After this, for all its friendliness, her voice was shot through with shadows.

Having captured equilibrium, Jan watched and listened in an attitude of ironic disinterestedness. He felt aloof, queerly superior, as if he were observing the three adults involved in a game of hopscotch or Rover Come Over. Well, let it come then, he thought.

In a while Uncle Hake departed, going off to his responsible job. The mother had telephoned for permission to come late to work, and she and Lora sat at the still-cluttered table conspiring like two secret agents. Often they clasped hands and protested mutual loving affection; their voices were sweet and twittery, excited, and yet the ground bass of vague sadness worked continuously beneath the sound, beneath both voices. Jan watched.

"Now Lora," the mother said, "there's no use in you and Hake spending good money to buy a house or, above all, paying rent. There's plenty of room right here in this house for all of us. Why, I'd just miss Hake terribly if he left—and I'd miss you too, you know I would." She patted her sister-in-law's freckled hand.

"Law, Miz Anderson, we couldn't hardly do that, to be in your way like that," Lora said.

"Now Lora, you call me Jenny, you're in the family now. I call you Lora, don't I?" the mother said.

"Well, all right then. Jenny," Lora said.

"No, it's a question of our being in your way. I can see that you-all would want to be alone, and I wouldn't want to put you in any situation that might cause you embarrassment," the mother said.

"There's not any trouble like that. I just wouldn't want to be in your way," Lora said.

(At the word "embarrassment" had Jan perceived a quick glance his way by his red-haired aunt?)

"You wouldn't be in my way at all. If you think you-all could be happy here I just wouldn't think of you-all going any place else," the mother said.

"Well, if we stayed on here you got to promise to let me keep up the housework just like I been doing. I mean, since I ain't got a job or anything. If we stayed, I wouldn't want to change anything from like the way it is, was," Lora said.

"Are you sure you'd want it that way?" the mother said.

"Yes mam. I sure don't want to lay around the house all day and not do nothing. I declare I believe Hake's lazy enough for both of us, the way it is already," Lora said.

The two women paused to smile.

"Call me Jenny, you don't have to call me mam. But now if you're sure you-all could be happy here, that would be fine. I think that what we want to do is just to exchange bedrooms. I'll take Hake's room, and you-all can move into the front bedroom," the mother said.

"I wouldn't put you out of your own room, not for anything in this world," Lora said.

"Why, you'll have to. You know yourself that that back bedroom's not large enough for two people, for you and Hake. And we won't have to move a thing, not a single piece of furniture. Just move my clothes and things in there, and put yours and Hake's things in the front bedroom," the mother said.

"I wouldn't put you out of your room, not for anything in this world," Lora said.

"Now Lora, I want you to have it. I wouldn't have it any other way, and I don't want you to say another word about it," the mother said.

She rose. The council was adjourned. They enlisted Jan's aid in carrying the mother's things into Uncle Hake's room and in carrying the old man's things out. They took everything: the thick packs of receipts, the pistol, the greasy clothing, even the pornographic volume from which both women turned away their ashamed eyes. Jan brought Lora's two big suitcases in from the front steps and stood awaiting instructions, holding the cases easily.

"Just put those wherever your aunt Lora tells you," the mother said.

He looked at his new kinswoman, who turned from arranging things in the tall maple chest of drawers. "I ain't going to call you Aunt," he said.

"Jan . . ." His mother's voice was almost breaking.

"That's all right," she said. "You just call me Lora, then."

He set the cases down and watched his mother going to prepare her make-up to go to work. When she entered Uncle Hake's dingy dark room her form seemed to be as dimmed and shadowed and lessened as if she were descending the obscurity of Avernus.

SIXTEEN

. . . AND LAY BACK gasping, indolently
pushing the love-wet stuffed giraffe away from her body.
The white forms of her intellect moved in an elegant
dance, adagio. What freedom!—brilliance of mind without responsibility, a condition of her nature which
matched the condition of natural eternity; the sea en-
tangled with the sun. At this moment, her blood sur-
feited with the acid juices of love, she felt that she need
never stir again. A giantess, she decided to permit all the
events in the universe, both the past and the future
events, to happen: to flow through her unseeming body
into history. From a cool enough perspective, all this flux

appeared to her a stillness. It was true, she had shut up all happening in a big bright box. She lifted her soft white hand, let it drop to the crumpled hot sheet.

All her foreseeing had drawn closer, everything which was about to happen was crowding to the needle's eye of her permitting. . . . And then what? There was a point past which she had no desire to look. At the time when the yellow stone golem crushed her brother to itself (that gelid heartless body) she covered away her seeing, as if she too had clapped on the blinding spectacles. After this oncoming moment she did not care, for it marked the completion of the whole history of Jan's love for her; it was to be killed by the instrument which had been constructed to guard it. She felt no pity for Jan because there was no fault in him. This outcome she herself determined—although at first she had been ignorant of it all—and she would not draw back. It was too fitting; the design pleased her, just as the inevitable design of a checkerboard might please her. Her vicious love of her brother rejoiced, whimpering.

Her breathing grew quieter, her soft white face relaxed. Her spirit nestled more hunched in that large body which personified satiety. The heavy odor of languor stuffed the little bedroom. She brushed her damp face. Everything was too clear to her; first the mother, her musky weightless presence sucked away into the air, and then Uncle Hake, whom it hardly seemed necessary to render inanimate because he had always so closely remained to that state, and then Jan, who had, almost from the beginning of his own memory, been willing himself out of being. Not all these terminations were deaths: they were just cancellations of comprehensible states of existence. Timmie felt no responsibility, none. Her mode of understanding was desire; she wasn't burdened with (or mastered by) will. Her body seemed to contract, to gain density by the coming on of sleep.

Her dream was at first filled with hands clamorous with beautiful wise weeping, the red mouths in the palms expressively open. The hands went about autonomously; there were no superfluous persons to chain them to dependence. They went round in different designs, a kaleidoscope of vocal hands. In the mouth of each hand bloomed a tiny red flower, each of which spoke also, in a different voice from the voice of the hand, a smaller voice and gentler. It was as if the sound of a violin contained a drawer which you could open to discover the sound of a harp. All the voices sang. These several voices became Jan's voice, not his own, but one which had attached to him, a high liquid treble capable of only a single deadly phrase: *crrooo, croo.* It was his eyes that were yellow now and the bird's body he inhabited had darkened, just as Jan's hair had darkened from the sugar-colored white to the dull glinty yellow, the color of tall sagegrass. The body of the fluffy pink bird had darkened to the color of a mouse; its yellow feral eyes were Jan's eyes; the bright bird had turned to an owl. It toppled forward from the spiny oak tree and came swooping low over the snow-smooth lawn. The sky was sunless, relentlessly gray with clouds, but the owl dropped on the ground a big shadow black as soot. Jan was frenzied. Jerking his thin body and waggling his arms he strove to protect his mother; and the owl veered away, sweeping effortlessly by the corner of the roof. *Croo.* It was useless. The black shadow had escaped the flight of the bird and it moved under its own power over the snow, over the front walk past Jan; seeped into the body of the poor mother. She stood silent and stoic as her white body turned the color of cigar ash, a gray the color of the sky. From her position high in the air Timmie observed it all. Jan was helpless. He turned to face the mother, but she did not speak, only gave him a long mournful unreproaching stare. He stepped toward her, but she gave him a forbidding shake of her head. Still silent, she turned her back on him and entered the house with a sad stately tread. He stood alone, glaring wildly to the east where the shape of the owl had got lost in the tangled top of leafless woods. Now the house was a different house, tall and hollow-looking, the seeing of the windows covered away by shutters. He stood, still staring. The dark attic window was momentarily paled by the white musky face of the mother. Jan went in. The house was creaky with cold air and emptiness. It was dingily dark. In room after room the wallpaper was ripped, showing shapes like weeping faces and like the faces of bats and wise mice. The sooty mouths of disused fireplaces whooped with the wind in the flues. In the corners were stubby fat reptiles whose bodies had hibernated but whose minds were alert and whose bitter eyes were open. The house boomed hollow all over with every step he took. . . . It was Jan's body, Jan's sensibilities, his fate in fact, but it was with Timmie's own perception that he saw. She was seeing for him now, exhibiting the bad future. . . . As he went up—and up and up—the stairs felt crumbling beneath his feet, and he could not gather the nerve to look behind; it seemed all too likely that the steps dissolved away as he ascended. The attic door would not take his key. He fumbled there for a long time, growing more frightened and exasperated, scarring the smug lock. He flung the key away and struck the door with his fists, but it was solid. He fancied he heard from inside a low female whisper. He smashed against the door with his thin shoulder, but it was solid. Turning about to descend he saw below only a series of dark vortices, yet he went down. The queasy stairs were littered with shards of bone, desiccated bits of gristle, scraps of paper with the halves of obscene words and of Jan's name torn away. And from the first floor floated up the sounds of something enormous painfully slithering over the cold rough boards and of huge deep breathing, the inhalation a suck half a minute long, a pause, and the exhaling a long low almost inaudible whistle.

She grinned, coming awake. She stretched her soft arms above her head. It was all so horridly true that she was almost happy. When Jan came next to visit her she would be silent and sympathetic. It was planned, it was planned and it was proper. This manner belonged to her now; it was she who held the fabric of his life in her mind; he would just have to get used to it. . . . She giggled. But of course he did not know, he could not guess the profound drift that event had taken: she was completely without responsibility.

She could not reconstruct in her head the old situation, in which the certainty of the stars in their courses had depended upon the strength of her brother. She could not conceive that things had ever happened in that manner. Maybe it was true that it had never been like that. She could easily think of a time in which she had, from the small bedroom and with the powerful aid of Jannie, guarded Jan, had staved off for a long while (now, of course, it was not possible) the encroachment of the extremity which his fierce will had brought upon him. Now it was impossible, she could not protect him, she was not responsible. She was, however, merciful. She had covered away his seeing with those square glasses; she had prevented him from seeing clearly, or even guessing clearly, what he was to bring upon himself. And too she had protected herself, from the moment in which those kindly blunt loving eyes would turn accusing upon her.

She moved in drowsy fervor, pulling her body to a sitting position in the bed. She rose unsteadily, the bare floor seemed to be dipping away from her, ebbing and dipping beneath her feet, swimming in her sight. Laying her hand on the head of the bed to steady herself, she considered. What did it mean, portend? It had nothing to do with her, it was what would happen to her brother. But she did not know when he would find the earth so unstable under him. There was nothing to discover; this knowledge came to her undesired; it was an intimation of a happening past the moment that she cared. She closed her eyes, opened them again. Things righted to equilibrium. . . . Poor Jan; she could not even fear the matter he was in for. Weary she was, frayed to the limits of her understanding. Long ago the ties of her pity had broken, like a rubber band stretched far past its elasticity. She could not even hope; foreknowledge erased the faintest vestiges of that mode of feeling. She went to the window and looked out at the July sunlight lying fat and self-sufficient in the smooth cropped lawn.

She was going to allow everything, to let it come down. She rejoiced and mourned at having it all so certain in the orderly pocket of her mind.

The moments were brittle with waiting; they would crush to powdery disaster. Everything was safe because inescapable. She placed the ear of her hand to her forehead and listened to the strong impartial voice of her knowing.

SEVENTEEN

THERE WAS a disease, of course, a secret cancer—it was not simply that Uncle Hake's dark old room had effaced the mother, obscuring her from existence like the bikinied lady in the photograph on the wall. This pin-up lady was now no more than indefinable outlines and a vague patch or two of light. The mother lay in the bed, growing weaker and so weightless that it seemed she might float off the bed and into the air. The doctors were pessimistic, but assertive: they did not give her much time, especially since she would not allow herself to be removed to a hospital. All the family was startled by her firmness upon this point; they had never suspected that she had anything of the adamant in her being.

The doctors consulted together in a corner of the living room. The younger man kept saying that it was incredible that this woman could not have observed her symptoms long before. Was she simply ignorant? Didn't these people know anything?

The older doctor, weary and paunchy, shook his head, nodded, shrugged. He rarely spoke except to the mother, whom he kept questioning in a gentle, almost listless voice.

Jan watched them both with eyes filled with suspecting hatred. He spent long days at his mother's bedside, not speaking. She lay quiet under his watching, occasionally smiling at him or asking for water or a handkerchief; she wanted some errand from him that might partially relieve his feelings. He stayed with her, silent, waiting, numb. She felt that he was more bewildered than frightened, and somehow it never occurred to her that her son had not expected this, her dying; he had always seemed to have everything well ordered in his head, resistless under his hand. She gazed at him as he sat continually by the foot of the bed. The dingy greasy room seemed to darken him also, even Jan. The small tears appeared and disappeared over all her face at regular intervals, like dew. When she spoke, her voice was slender and fragile as the thread of a cobweb. "Jan . . ."

"Yes?"

"Nothing. Nothing, darling."

His stiff eyes rested on her face. She almost giggled, she felt so secure in his presence. Hadn't he always taken care of Timmie in just this manner? Hadn't he always been unassailable? It was no wonder the daughter had become so dependent upon him; the person that he was allowed for no other possibility. His protection was so perfect it was killing. . . . Poor Timmie . . . The mother went to great lengths to keep from trying to think about what would happen to the family when she was gone. It seemed that something would: Jan, and even his sister, carried in themselves an air of resigned waiting, of the expectancy of something terrifying. But when she remembered how their lives had been, she could not think how her absence would make much difference. There would be weeping, of course—she knew that she was loved by them—but hadn't she always really been absent? First sealed away by grief for her dead Robert, and then by Jan's stubborn independence of her, and by Timmie's dependence upon her brother. If there had actually ever been a time when an act of love on her part would have made their lives different, would have drawn the three, or the four, of them closer, there had never been an arena where such an act could take place, not even an interstice where it could jam through. This sort of speculation left her ever more weary; the almost buoyant body seemed burdensome, and her spirit almost retired from it, would effuse through the pores of her fair skin.

She looked at Jan sitting, tortured and unmoving, at the foot of the bed, and she again experienced the impulse to laugh. Her poor pitied intense son, by virtue of his very intensity a bit pompous, a bit like his Uncle Hake. There was too much irony in this impression for her to trust it: that Jan, who was almost selfless, should come to resemble his almost totally selfish uncle whom he despised—it was really too perverse. Jan had had the air of importance thrust upon him, while unfortunate Hake had conjured it out of his own misplaced self-esteem. It was not fair to Jan, but she couldn't help the urge to

124

giggle. She thought that she ought really to give to her son some solemn deathbed advice, some important final injunction, but she couldn't think of anything. What was he waiting down there for anyway, motionless as a stone idol? Don't push no ducks in the pond: her brother's favorite piece of advice came into her head, and she finally had to let the light laugh utter itself.

But it came out as a croaking murmur, and Jan's eyes veered to her face. Obviously she had frightened him. "Jan," she said.

"Yes," he said.

"Would you please bring me a glass of water?"

He rose with a single motion and went to the door.

"And . . ."

He turned, waiting for the rest of her request.

"And would you mind putting on your glasses?"

He gave a short nod and when he returned with the dripping glass his blunt eyes were hidden by the white patches of the reflecting lenses. Because she had asked for it she had to take a few sips of the tepid water, but she was really grateful that he had covered away his disturbing eyes; waiting with her son in a bare room to die, she felt there was no reason she had to put up with that troubling gaze now.

And now her sister-in-law had come in to keep company with her, and she wished she hadn't asked Jan to wear those worthless glasses. She wanted to see how Jan would look at Lora. There was something going on, yes, on both sides between them. And now she realized she hoped it was sexual desire; she had never noticed that Jan had ever desired anything for himself. It was for Timmie he had always wanted. Of course this present wanting could not come to fruition because of that stupid

125

marriage, but she was happy to think that it was there, that there was a chance for Jan to get into a world larger than this house and that abandoned barn. What had he always been doing in that barn? Long ago she ought to have visited it.

The red-haired girl bent over her with studied tenderness. "Is there anything I can do for you, Jenny? Is there anything you want?"

"No. No thank you," she said. The words cost her much strength. What she wanted from Lora was once again to be addressed as Mrs. Anderson, but that time was gone forever. Once more, an impulse to laugh: yes, really forever. It seemed to the mother that she had not truly come to death, she had merely been displaced.

Lora moved gently and spoke tenderly, but there was nothing tender behind those luminous green eyes: there was a bright steady impersonal light there. "Are you feeling better?"

"Yes," she said, "I feel better." Until she spoke, she hadn't realized that she would whisper. There was no strength at all in her throat.

"I'm sure you do," she said. "I was just telling Hake this morning how much better you was looking, and he said he thought so too. I guess it won't be any time at all now before you get your strength back and be up and around. It'll be before you know it, any time at all now, I bet a nickel." She looked at Jan, who was again seated at the foot of the bed. "Ain't that so, Jan?"

He didn't assent, didn't move a muscle.

Even if she could not see Jan's expression, there was no mistaking the intent in Lora's brilliant green gaze. There were designs, determined plans, in that red-haired head, ideas so defined as to be almost already accomplished.

Did he know? It would be strange if he didn't, but now she felt that she would like to comfort him as she had used to be able to comfort his sister, to draw him to her fatal chest and babble out the warm nonsense: "There there, darling, there now, sweetheart, there-there." Suddenly those words seemed the one act of love she had ever rendered her beautiful children; it was no wonder she had been displaced from this world. Her removal was something that calculation and energy could execute quite accidentally, without motion diverted from its original course. Somehow the wasting of her own life had at some point got to be a necessity to her.

Lora was still running on. "And I said I bet we'll see Jenny up and about in the springtime; she'll be up to see the flowers and the trees and all come out in the springtime. When the weather gets warm after this coming winter I bet she'll chirk up and be as frisky as a puppy dog, that's what I told him and he thought I was right, every word I said. . . ."

What was this jabber all about? Lora's voice diminished to a pinpoint of sound and then expanded like a balloon filling with air and then leaked away again like water swirling down the drain of a sink. The mother felt she was sinking with this floating feeling; she would like to cut loose the bindings. The dark room was flooded with burning light, and she thought she could no longer restrain her laughter, a soundless giggling which suffused her weariness with a crazy glittering spumescence. She understood that the string of cool gibberish was not directed toward herself but toward her blinded Jan. And she was entirely helpless, clenched convulsively in her body with silent unexpressive laughing.

On and on. "Such a fine wonderful WOMAN AS JENNY

is, she'll soon be AROUND. A FINE lady like that, you JUST CAN'T keep her down. And you know HAKE HE DON'T talk much but you CAN TELL WHAT he's thinking and HE THOUGHT I was right every WORD. . . ."

Her whole frame ached with the effort of restraining her laughter; she stiffened.

"And I was thinking maybe we could put a bed or two of flowers right outside the living-room windows there where you could see them any time you wanted, and then we could have flowers for the house. They're cheerful, I think, flowers, they actually sort of keep a body company. . . ."

Jan rose from his chair and went to the head of the bed. With a calm careful hand he brushed away every tiny tear from the mother's unmoving face. He gave her a steady look and then pulled the dingy sheet up over her face.

"Oh Lord," said Lora, "oh my God. I didn't even—I didn't know she had . . . was . . . ."

Hunched forward with his hands in his pockets, Jan left the dark room without a sound.

EIGHTEEN

TIMMIE OF COURSE could not, Jan would not, attend the funeral. Nothing could persuade him. Uncle Hake and Lora found it even more difficult than before to guess the violent thoughts in Jan's intent head—Jan himself did not know what he thought. Everything had changed; not even the physical world had remained true for him. It was as if his mother's death had opened, not closed, a door, a portal entering upon maze upon maze of blind queasy corridors he could not escape. Every extra-personal object seemed flimsy, gelatinous. He moved hesitantly and slowly, as if the air itself weighed too much, a breathable water. In his mind things were in pieces.

No peace, no peace from Uncle Hake. "Ungrateful?" he said. "My God. After all that poor woman done for you to go and treat her like that, not to even go to her funeral . . . My God, a feller that won't go to his own mother's funeral."

"Hush," Jan said. "Hush up." In his poor head was the onset of the migraine headache which would never leave him. His brain felt like an arm or a leg in which the circulation of the blood has been stopped by a tied cord.

The old man retreated, muttering and cursing, chewing at the frizzly corner of his mustache.

But, after all, it was just as well that Jan didn't attend the funeral. Timmie couldn't be left alone in the house, and Lora was going to the funeral service, but not to the graveyard. She explained that she couldn't bear the interring. "Hake, I just couldn't stand it, after all that poor woman . . . I just couldn't stand it, to go out there and see them throw that dirt on top of poor Jenny. I know I just couldn't stand it." But as she talked, those thinking verdant eyes rested on Jan's averted face. In that gaze was foreseeing, of an animal order.

Uncle Hake acquiesced tenderly; he could understand that a woman was soft, sentimental, and there was Jan's attitude before him as contrast. Lora was to return from church in the car, and he would get a ride back from the graveyard with a friend or with the minister. The kids would remain at home. God only knew what people—the friends he had to look in the face every day—would say about that, but what could he do? Jenny, bless her soul, had already spoiled them rotten, and he certainly couldn't teach them respect in a couple of hours. For later, however, he had disciplinary plans.

He waited for Lora impatiently, pacing about the house. He had loved—in his way—his sister; he wanted to get it over with. The longer the mother stayed aboveground the more uncomfortable he was.

Now the delay was caused by a zipper in Lora's dark-gray suit. She came to the bedroom door and asked, her voice impaled by three bobby pins clenched in her teeth, for Uncle Hake's assistance. At her hip the skirt flapped open, showing a smooth bulging triangle of her pink slip. Again her gaze sought Jan; she made certain that Jan saw the faulty zipper. Which couldn't have been very much out of order, for even clumsy Uncle Hake zipped it up tight—Jan didn't even perceive that he was being watched.

At last they departed. Jan watched the car pull away. It was early October. In the mountains the maple leaves were scarlet, the beech trees were erect and mobile like yellow fingers. A sharp breeze made the air effervescent, and in this brittle pureness the mountains seemed to have floated forward, nearer now in the absence of the summer haze. The mountains were blue and green and blue-green, spattered occasionally with yellow and red. The sky was clear as a lens of the spectacles he wore. Warm weather, but the breeze was edged, bearing already the imminence of winter.

He sat on a couch in the living room for a long time. He thought and thought. Then he went into the kitchen and poured a glass of milk and drank half of it. On the drainboard of the sink lay a small paring knife, the blade flecked with bits of potato peeling. He almost gathered up the knife from force of habit before he recalled that he no longer had to do this; Timmie was kept locked in her room now. Needles, scissors, and knives lay scattered all about the house. But he couldn't subdue the involuntary muscle of habit: he still looked all about the house to protect her, like a military commander inspecting on the eve of a grand defensive maneuver. And now, what at last was there to protect her from? She was safe from Uncle Hake or Lora, safe now from everyone. Jan suspected irony in his sister's watching him. Wasn't she now finally simply more intelligent than he, even though her intelligence was suffused with the demoniac? He set the half-filled glass of milk on the drainboard and went down the hall to Timmie's room. The house was charged with waiting; it felt heavy and expectant on his skin. His headache rang like cold iron.

He unlocked the door and entered. His sister stood with her back to him, looking out the window to the sun-drenched lawn. She hummed in her light voice a timeless wordless song. Now she was happy, and Jan supposed that she didn't understand what had happened, that the mother had died. He thought that Timmie could not imagine an eternal departure, but he forced himself to remember his sister's new nature—her old naked innocence was gone, or had become bitter. Jan was utterly confused; he forced a smile on his tight face.

But when she turned and saw that he was smiling she began to frown. Was it anger? He could not know; his face became grave and taut again, and his sister smiled gaily. All this was unfair; she knew too much her advantage, his unceasing fear for her, and she pressed ruthlessly. But he felt that she did not entirely hate him.

"Timmie . . ."

She made a light pirouette, holding her skirt up about her knees.

He shrugged. "Do you want me to read you a story?" he asked. He was helpless.

She went round and round to an inaudible waltz measure. "Mother." She almost sang the word, but her voice was clear, assertive.

"Timmie . . ."

"She's just bones now. Isn't she just a big pile of bones? I bet I know."

"No. She's all right. It's all right now."

"Mice," she said.

"There ain't no mice."

"Was mice," she said. "You talk just like the mice, I can tell."

It was true. Each time he opened his mouth dozens of tiny gray mice squirmed out and tumbled to the floor; ran scrabbling about the room. *Keek. Keek, keerk, keerk. Keerk. Keek.*

"There ain't no mice," he said.

But it was true; it was because Jan used to bite mice. Their eyes were bad, glowing like bloody stars. "The mice made her just like a big pile of bones. I can tell."

"No, Timmie, there's not any mice. She's all right, it's all right now."

She frowned heavily and turned from him. Jan's hair had got dark yellow and he was blinded by the glasses. He wasn't like Jan at all but like a dark stain in the grainy wood of a door. Everything about her brother was diminished now, and the time that mattered was dwindling. She couldn't prevent her condescension; she knew too much. "Are you going to read me about Peter Rabbit?"

He stood transfixed for a moment. Whole dimensions of heat and cold seemed to move through his body. He was shivering, gooseflesh made the sparse blond hairs on the backs of his hands tall and brittle. The migraine was heavy and solid, like a full rank cabbage. "I will in just a minute," he said. He went out the door and down to the hall closet. From a peg he took his tan windbreaker that had faded from rain and wind to a yellow color just slightly darker than his hair. He got into it and zipped it up. He still felt cold.

When she heard him coming back down the hall she stepped silently back from the doorknob she had been trying to ease over without noise. She had heard that he hadn't locked it; he had forgot. And why shouldn't she have her freedom? She knew more than anyone, she was entirely free except for the locked door. He entered with a forced cheerful air, and she kept stepping backward away from him.

"Let's see now," he said. "Where's that Peter Rabbit book at?" He located it without difficulty and delivered it to the bed. He sat on the edge and patted the space beside him where two pillows were piled against the headboard. "Why don't you come over here and lay down where you can hear?" he said. Still cold, he turned up the collar of his jacket.

Jannie was tumbled in a corner, his spectacled eye spaces turned to the wall. She gathered the toy to her soft breasts as if it were not inert, but a breathing being. She came docilely to the bed, lay back and watched Jan as he opened the thin book. His hands were frightened of her, trembled like mice.

"Once . . . Once . . ." His voice was squeaky with mice. Two times he had to clear his throat. "Once upon a time there were four little Rabbits, and their names were—Flopsy, Mopsy, Cotton-tail, and Peter."

She reached over his scared hands and turned three, four pages until she found Mr. McGregor, who was on his hands and knees planting out young cabbages. Mr. McGregor was frightened behind his beard, and his eyes were blinded, covered away by the white glasses like Jan's.

He obediently began reading in this place. "Peter was most dreadfully frightened; he rushed all over the garden, for he had forgotten the way back to the gate."

She poked the picture of the old man with a direct finger. "He can't see anything. He can't know," she said. "I covered up his eyes so he can't see."

"Those are his glasses, so he can see better."

Her triumph was almost spectacular. She was happy; remained firm. "No, I covered up his eyes so he can't see."

He read on rapidly. He was cold and she embarrassed him. "Mr. McGregor was quite sure that Peter was somewhere in the toolshed, perhaps hidden underneath a flower-pot. He began to turn them over carefully, looking under each." Perhaps it was the story which made Jan feel so silly.

Again she put her finger on the old man. "See how he can't see? I covered up his eyes. He can't see where Peter Rabbit is."

"No," he said. "He won't find Peter Rabbit. You have to be quiet now, so I can read to you."

She snuggled down obediently, clutching Jannie more tightly to her. She seemed light, happy, dreamy, certain.

Jan read on to the end: "But Flopsy, Mopsy, and Cot-

ton-tail had bread and milk and blackberries for supper."
He felt silly. His headache had become worse.

Timmie was suddenly asleep. Her soft heavy face
moved slowly to smile, the mood of her dreaming passing
over it like a breeze moving over a pool of water. Very
carefully he brushed a film of dark hair back off her
forehead. He would have liked to know what she was
dreaming, what images appeared to her sleeping mind to
make her happy. It was hard to believe that she really
understood that the mother had died, but she was obviously satisfied that she understood. And what if she did?
. . . It frightened him to think that his sister might be
made happy by a death, that her perverseness had gained
so much of her. It would be impossible to know how far
her perverseness went. . . . Did she really know her
loss? He preferred to think she did not, that she stayed
safe inside her delusions. Poor Timmie was not so poor
after all.

—Or he was mistaken, and it was the loss of the
mother that moved her to gaiety. He couldn't understand. She must have, she had loved her mother. It was
simply that events had for Timmie values which he did
not perceive. It was as if she were playing a chess game
with pieces whose shapes were utterly foreign to him.
There was, however, a certain complacency, actually a
smugness, on her side which made Jan suffer to know
what his sister knew, or imagined that she knew.

A dry burning sensation beneath his eyes. If he had
known how, he would have wept. This he could not remember ever having done: it was like making a joke, it
was useful, but he simply did not comprehend the
mechanics of the act. He rubbed his smarting eyes into
the shoulder of his windbreaker. He lay beside his sister

for a long time, poring over his thoughts. She lay with her mouth slightly opened; under her slow breathing he discovered that, asleep, she was humming a wordless tuneless song.

He had heard no one enter the house, so that he started slightly when he heard the faint rap at the bedroom door. He lay still for a moment, trying to see if his sudden movement had waked Timmie. The light hesitant tapping sounded again.

"Jan, are you in there?"

It was his aunt Lora, speaking quietly, her voice dull, as if it were swathed in the presence of the door. He rose from the bed as cautiously as if there were a house of cards stilted there that he mustn't topple; opened the door noiselessly.

She stood before him, her hand uplifted to rap once more. Her face was hot. She was wearing the skirt of the dark-gray suit, but she had divested herself of the suit jacket. On her torso was a pink slip, vague at the edges with a light frothy lace. Her voice was scratchy in the whisper. "Could you help me a minute, Jan?" she said. She stepped back.

He came into the hall, slipping the door closed behind him: carefully, carefully. He removed from his face the unmagnifying square spectacles, pushed them into the pocket of his windbreaker.

Now that his eyes were bared, she blushed even more under his vehement stare; placed her hand high on her chest dotted with rosy freckles; moved her hand to stroke her neck nervously. "It's just this silly zipper," she said, "I can't get it undone. . . ." Her voice was still hushed and tight.

He gave a wordless nod, almost imperceptible.

137

Her observed skin was still fiery red, and she turned and went down the hall to the front bedroom. He followed at a short distance, still mute. It seemed she was receding, wraithlike, down the gloomy tunnel of his migraine. She entered the bright room, she seemed floating. She stopped at the right side of the bed and turned her left hip toward it; indicated that he was to sit on the bed. "I just had an awful time before we left with this silly thing," she said. "And I finally had to get Hake to give me some help. I can't understand what's got wrong with it."

He sat on the edge of the bed, very slowly letting his weight settle. He didn't want to disturb his head.

Lora seemed unearthly.

But there was nothing wrong with the zipper; it moved steadily on its ripe track. Slowly and smoothly the dark skirt slid down her hips. "Well, I declare," she said. She was fantastic, her voice was filled with the yellow glare of triumph. She stepped daintily out of the puddle of cloth, bent and picked the skirt up; gazed at the zipper with ostentatious interest. "Well, I don't see why I couldn't get it to work like that."

Beneath the windbreaker heavy globules of sweat rolled down his chest. He couldn't believe in her existence. He seemed to be clawing for breath: maybe it was the perfume, fat, summery.

She flung the skirt away.

She stood steady in her slip, which was edged again at the bottom with the frothy lace. It seemed that the lace was the visual image of all that warm perfume. She wore high-heeled black patent-leather shoes. He placed his fingertips on the smooth outer curve of her hip.

She took his face in her cold hands, turned it one way

and then another, as if she were considering it as purchasable merchandise. Migraine flamed and sputtered like a gas jet.

It seemed that he could put his hands through her, as through steam. Her hip was warm in both his hands. Her calm cold hands restrained without repulsing.

She stood barefoot on the small light-blue rug. The soles of her feet were tough and yellow. She stood steady in her panties and brassière; her slip was flung near her skirt, a small gray-and-pink pool, sweet-smelling, warm. Her ankles and calves were slim, but her hams were large and muscular. "Well," she said. "Well I declare." Her voice was stuffy with triumph.

She sat naked on the edge of the bed, her feet not quite touching the floor, and her body looked as if it were leaning heavily outside itself. She wiggled her toes like a swimmer uncertain whether to enter a cold pool. Her cheerful breasts were wide apart; the clay-colored nipples were sealed but observant eyes. She was giggling, her soft unfreckled belly jiggled merrily. "It's *cool*," she said. "I'm cold." Between her legs foamed the full V of red hair, and her sex was a coy sticky sidewise wink.

His body was running with sweat heavy as syrup. Between Lora and his vision were illusory layers of film, and all strength had seeped out of him, washed away indistinguishably in the waves of her steamy perfume. It had washed his head clean of every other impression. He could not decide where his body was, trapped and smothered in his clothing; his chest was like a choked sob. She was giggling; now she was laughing at him full out, but the sound seemed far distant because of the roaring of the wild blood in his ears. He tottered forward, coming around the edge of the bed. Now her hands were warm; she was still giggling, and she unbound his body from the stifling cloth.

The migraine was tautly crouched like a big yellow animal.

It was like drifting slowly down through tepid water.

NINETEEN

Now she had him, he couldn't stir without her allowing. He was like an empty eggshell that she kept rolling gently to and fro under her instep. Everything at last—his whole being—had betrayed him into her hands; and although it seemed that this pattern of living wouldn't go on for very long, Jan had no thoughts about the future.

Lora worked as usual about the house, cheerful, often singing. Now it was almost her house alone, and she kept it fresh as new linen. Treated Uncle Hake with a show of great tenderness and concern; left Timmie almost completely alone, as if the girl was an unnecessary bother; smiled quaintly at Jan—when she saw him—and sometimes snapped him a quick wink. She appeared to be as single in purpose and as successful as a machine.

Most of the day she did not see Jan. He continued to skip breakfast, and then he was in school. When he came home he occupied himself with Timmie, or spent slow aching hours in the barn. But by four o'clock he had always wandered brokenly to the door of the bright front bedroom where Lora awaited him, sitting on the wide bed, naked but for a robe. She smiled saturninely as he entered.

She treated him like a dog that she liked pretty well, or sometimes like an invalid, which he mostly was. The pain inside his skull was like fingers intermittently grasping. Often he had to lean against walls and fight for breath; air seemed as hard as ice to get into the lungs. But he knew what it was, even underneath the migraine his intellect could still at times flare brightly: motive had snapped within him; he found nothing to care about. He fed his appetite, which had not much hunger. He didn't care, but as long as there was the semblance of a shadow of necessity, he would move toward the repairing of it. And although he knew that he was accepting the counterfeit, there seemed nothing else to act for.

He truly couldn't understand why she wanted him. She did not want him; she treated him with condescension, with an air of weary tolerance, and she fostered in him the impression of his excruciating inadequacy. And the whole black world she had discovered to him horrified him simply; he was not constructed for desire; his mind demanded singleness, and in love, in lust, there was only bewildering multiplicity and ambiguity. Jan could not imagine a thing without use, and he could not

142

imagine what use he was to his aunt. His will he still retained; he carried it about like a very heavy pistol with the hammer spring broken. More and more he fed upon the lust of impotence.

Lora asked him, "What are you going to be when you grow up?" She lay on her side, watching him wrestle into his clothes, her arm tucked under her red hair. He was frightened to look at her.

This situation obtained for about two weeks, and all this time his body was painful.

TWENTY

AND THEN AT LAST they were discovered, though
not in the manner Lora had planned. All this unlooked-
for desire had kept working at, had sapped, Jan's vigi-
lance, which had come to feel to him unnecessary and,
at last, onerous. He had forgot to lock Timmie's door
after a session with her and Peter Rabbit; he had wandered away almost like an automaton, treading the tense
febrile path to his aunt's bedroom.

She sat with her legs crossed beneath her on the bed;
naked under her careless yellow house robe she seemed
an exotic idol. In the doorway he paused, nodded shortly
to her as if in obeisance, and she laughed.

"How-di-do," she said.

He paused still. Oh, was today going to be one of her cruel laughing days? He winced under the memory of her scarlet fingernails, busy on his flesh in jollity.

"What are you waiting for?" she asked. Her body was open in the open robe, and candid, heartbreaking.

The migraine moved in his head as he moved slowly forward. His body was hesitant, his fear precipitant. He did not understand her; she was too much an object, and yet not actual at all. There was not enough matter about her to fix his will upon.

He stripped off his shirt, the act familiar, unthinking.

Perhaps all his aunt was, finally, was this animal laughter, habitual too and too unthinking. There was nothing in her which suggested consciousness, but only cunning, wild and bright-eyed. And yet she was wrong to laugh like that, with her eyes fearful and her mouth taut and round with fear. It was another proof of her lack of actuality, this contradiction in her attitude and her gestures. It was proof she wasn't real.

The blood made his hand slippery on the bedpost; he could not hold it; it slipped from his grasp. His hand was numb from Lora's mindless laughing. His hand was weighty as a stone, willess as a doorknob. He shuddered like a candle flame as he plucked the paring knife from his hand. The short blade was unwashed, smeared slightly with yellow mustard. As he watched, his hand glowered, becoming red. His face was beaded with sweat as he turned, and the turning took all his strength.

"Timmie," he said.

She kept laughing louder and louder and happier. It was all too true, it was absurd. It was as she had known.

When she uncovered, opened the mouth of his hand it issued a chorus of red voices. They spoke to her in a loud clever jangle, confirming everything. It was all too true, it was as she had known. She wished only that Jan would cover his bad eyes. Where were the glasses she had made him wear? Now he was angry; he would find her beneath the flowerpot, and with his long rake he would stroke all her long pretty hair off. Only this was not as she had permitted. She felt she ought to run from him, lippity-lippity, but she would not; she was still too happy.

He flung the knife into a corner. The blood ran in streamlets down the bedpost and shone in bright patches on the white chenille. His hand was an alien object; it fought his will successfully. "Timmie," he said, "you got to go back. We got to go back to your room." She was like his aunt, she was all contradiction: now she had stopped laughing, and she uttered a scream through her happy smile; and in her eyes was a victorious expression. . . . —It was not his sister. No. It was Lora who was screaming. Screech, screech. She had fallen back against the headboard of the bed, her eyes wide, protuberant. She clutched the robe tightly around her; fear had accomplished what shame could not: she had gagged her body. Her throat was loud. "Shut up," he said. "Shut up that goddam screeching."

With his unwounded left hand he led Timmie from the room, down the hall. "I was bad, wasn't I? Wasn't I real bad, Jan? I wasn't just joking, was I? I was real bad."

"Yes," he said. "You were real bad, Timmie. That was a bad thing to do." He couldn't understand why this comforted her. His head raged.

When they entered her room she ran immediately to

146

Jannie. She began to gnaw and suck the worn stuffed head. She watched Jan with eyes as bright and tough as a bird's. "There's red mice on the floor," she said. Her voice was observant, speculative.

He looked: it was true. His blood had formed a mouse-shaped stain on the streaked pine. "Now, you stay here and be good now. Because you've been bad." He felt that there was something urgent to be done about Lora, but he didn't know what. He couldn't hear her screeching now, but the urge to hurry was undeniable. "You'll be good now, won't you? Timmie?" He kept all foreboding out of his voice.

She advanced, holding the toy giraffe up to him. "Give Jannie a kiss," she said. "Give Jannie a nice kiss so it will make me be good."

He leaned, kissed perfunctorily the greasy forehead of the toy. Immediately she began to laugh in cold delight.

He backed away from her slowly and went out. He locked the door. It didn't matter; she stood still in the center of the room, laughing.

He was stunned; his whole being seemed deafened, mute, blind. He stood lost in the hallway, halted, it seemed to him, in the act of stepping back from the door of Timmie's bedroom. He had lost time; in these instants he felt drawn out of duration, upended like a newborn child—the gauzy stuff that sequence was made of was distant. His own thinking was remote from him, and he considered the checkered patterns of his perception coldly and with distaste. But pain did not leave him. The migraine plumed itself, spreading open like a peacock in strut, and his arm was livid with the pain in his hand. It seemed the two hurts would join, Alpheus and Arethusa in arcane coition. —And then, with resolve and

147

deliberation, he stepped back into time. He felt firm.

All too late. Uncle Hake rushed to fill the doorway to the front bedroom. His greasy face was red and angry as an explosion; it looked as if it might pop loose from his neck. He fought in vain to talk. At his side he held the heavy pistol, and behind him Jan watched Lora struggling to hurry into her clothes. She kept dropping her panties and picking them up again. Her body shuddered with her breathing.

"Such a goddam son of a bitch . . ."

Uncle Hake brought the pistol muzzle to bear upon Jan's forehead. "Goddam son of a bitch," he said. "You goddam son of a bitch." He pulled the trigger twice. Three times, four times. There was the mere flat sound of the revolver hammer burying itself in the wooden bullets. He gave the pistol a stupid stare, holding it loose in his open hand, waist high. "You goddam son of a bitch," he said. His voice was low, without an edge, weary; Uncle Hake seemed exhausted. He dropped the gun on the hall floor, slammed shut the door. "Get some goddam clothes on." Jan heard him through the door.

Slowly and with great care, Jan bent and picked up the pistol. What had Lora told his uncle? Even now he could not guess her purposes, he could not try. What was important was that he had been shot: four unreal bullets had zipped through his brain. He had underestimated his uncle, or, rather, he had not estimated him at all. What about Timmie? He shrugged. Uncle Hake had tried to kill him.

He bore the pistol before him like a votive offering, holding it gently in his left hand. His right hand sprinkled blind spots of blood behind each step he took. At the hall closet he stopped and took out his faded yellow windbreaker and put it on. He was not cold, but he felt vaguely that the rough closeness of the jacket would comfort his abrased body. Slouched, huddled in himself, entirely painful, he went out to the barn, entered the old stall, leaned for a while against the wall. He was weak, everything he saw was palpitant. He rolled his head against the unfriendly boards, rolled his eyes. Abruptly he stood straight, not again would he drift out of temporality. He crossed the stall and opened the converted chest. He took three pistol bullets from a jar lid where they had been lying in a film of oil. Perhaps they wouldn't fire; they were very old. He opened the cylinder of the pistol and lifted the wooden bullets out with his fingernails. To the firing pin was stuck a wadlet of mixed clay and fingernail polish, the phony cap he had made for the wooden bullets. Now at last he had got calm and steady; his mind seemed clear as ice. He cleaned the hammer and loaded the pistol; looked about him at the stall, the hollow barn, as if taking farewell.

He went back to the house and stood before the bedroom door. He could hear Uncle Hake still cursing, haranguing red-haired Lora. He watched the door, calculating where Uncle Hake's heart would be when the door was opened. Then he knocked, lightly. "Hey," he said. His voice was cool and unwavering. "Hey, in there." The heavy steps advanced to the door, and it opened. He had figured correctly. He shot his uncle twice through the heart.

The bullets were old and the shots were so loud that they seemed to hang palpable in the air like two big black bubbles. The old man fell backward instantly, like a chair tipped over. He said nothing, but vocal red blood welled from his mouth, clutched his throat like a hand. Lora was screaming and screaming. Didn't she ever shut up? "Hush up that goddam screeching," Jan said. With his foot he pushed Uncle Hake's dead legs away and closed the door.

His right hand still bled, the ache of it spurted in his arm, a blazing fountain. He went into the bathroom, dropped the pistol into the lavatory and ran warm water over his hand. He had kicked his uncle's legs out of the way like empty bottles, had closed the door, a final refusal. What was the sound that had come through the shut door? Was it Lora gagging, or was it Uncle Hake's body, already ripping asunder with its charged corruption? The water turned pink from his hand and splashed on the gun. He opened the medicine chest and found a roll of gauze and wrapped it clumsily over the palm of his hand and then he got the bottle of alcohol and poured it over the bandage, wincing slightly at the smart. Here was Uncle Hake's bottle of whiskey. He unscrewed the cap and took a long swallow; shivered, from the base of his spine up. It tasted bad, burning and musty and sweetish. He took it away with him. He imagined in the bedroom Uncle Hake's body lying burst like a balloon, nerve and gut exposed to the objective light. He wiped his mouth on the shoulder of his jacket.

He could not return to the barn to think. He trudged slowly down the hall, and he thought that he might look in on Timmie. He slipped on the steel-rimmed spectacles, but then decided not to go in; he heard no sounds from inside. The house was mute except for his own jagged breathing, his breathing. He went out the back door and across the smooth lawn. In the breeze the oak branches stirred fitfully. Crossing the ditch carefully he went up into the field of sagegrass. He found a place and sat squatting on his heels, unmoving for a long time, except occasionally to take swallows from the bottle.

He waited for things to make sense.

The sun was high and hot and white. The sky was clear as a lens, polished by the admonitory wind.

He was drunk. In the yellowed windbreaker his chest swam in sweat. The hair at the back of his neck was damp and itchy with sweat. His darkened hair was the same bright yellow as the sagegrass. In the unmagnifying spectacles the reflected sagegrass was worried over by the wind. In each glass square the reflected sun was a tiny yellow dot, the size of the pupils of his eyes. His mind was clear of everything but the yellow light and his own presence. All past happening had removed, receded, diminished in his being to a single pinpoint of blackness. He existed so weightily in the field that he might have created it. At the back of his neck the muscles distended to the size of fingers when he tipped back his head to drink. He drank again and again.

The migraine had only a tenuous connection with his head. Now it had couched itself in a round whitish stone which lay on the ground a yard or so before him, a stone about the size of, the color of, a baseball. He watched it intensely, thinking that perhaps the object could efface him, for it too was hugely self-willed. It contested heartily his supremacy of existence in this yellow field, and now he remembered it perfectly. It was a baseball— he remembered it perfectly; had come spinning, fouled back, arcing up over the ditch and over the sagegrass. In the worn baseball was its deliberate power to forget him out of being, and it fell thumping and rolled softly forward, coming to rest a yard or so before him. In its flight it had dropped no shadow on the ground.

The couple, the little boy and girl, went down into the

trickling ditch; bobbed up again like divers. The boy was looking for the baseball; holding his sister's hand, he made wide arcs in the field, going back and forth and looking about his feet for the ball. In the sunlight his sugar-colored hair caused silver circles to spread over the air. He spoke quiet comforting words to the girl, calming her as one would calm an animal, and she clutched his hand, looking tightly at his intent face.

He held the bottle without drinking; he had forgot his wounded right hand. He watched the ball. They were going to find it, but still they had not seen him. He stood quickly, too quickly, for he almost toppled from the whiskey. He towered over them, and he looked wild and yellow, his darkened yellow hair, his faded jacket. They stared at his red right hand, and he eased the bottle carefully into it, bent and scooped the ball and held it over his head. He squeezed the ball so tightly that his arm shook. He wanted to squeeze the ball to a powder.

It had all gone wrong, and he knew urgently that he ought to warn them. He ought to admonish this Jan, to preach to him. But meaning clotted in his mind. His mind was seared yellow with the drinking, and words sputtered and sizzled away like water drops in a hot frying pan. The ball shook in his hand; he looked wild and yellow. The boy and girl retreated a few steps, the boy dragging the girl back, getting her behind himself. They were both white and so fearful they might have trembled out of existence, like match flames.

The words would not form in his head. "Hanh!" he cried. "You goddam kids! What if you was to die? What if you was to die one day?"

The white-haired boy looked so fierce from fear that he looked like a trapped fox.

"Jan. Ja-an," she said. Her voice was fragile as a silk thread.

"One day; what if you was to die one day?" he cried. "Hanh! Hanh!" He threw the ball away into the lawn, and it rolled forward, bouncing against the oak tree. "Hanh! Hanh!" And here it was at last, a joke: it bloomed before him in incredible brilliance and variegation, held unnumbered light shadows; and at last he laughed. He was laughing and shouting. *Hanh.*

He walked toward them and they did not run. But they receded, as if they were floating away down a corridor of splintered mirrors. He passed them by, and they were not there; he had turned a big invisible corner of the airy light and he was out of sight of them. He stopped to shift the bottle into his unwounded left hand. He drank; there was not much left. He needed to conserve what flamed in the sunlit bottle, fired his throat. The sky reeled, world roiled shockingly in the drunkenness. He was still laughing, and when he came to the bank of the roadbed he was laughing so hard he could not walk up, he had to go down on his hands and knees —careful, careful with the bottle—and crawl. He reached the road and stood. He drank once more; tipped his head far back, as if he were swallowing the light and heat of the sun. He began walking. Beneath his confused feet the earth ebbed and swayed, as it might ebb and sway below the feet of a man who had been hanged.

$\mathcal{V}$OICES OF THE $\mathcal{S}$OUTH